The Ghost
of Spirit River

The Ghost
of Spirit River

JEANNE DIXON &
BRADFORD ANGIER

drawings by E. Carey Kenney

ATHENEUM   1968   New York

for JAMES PAIGE DIXON

The Ghost
of Spirit River

SECOND CABIN

LAKE

FIRST CABIN

WATER FALLS

HELLGATE CANYON

FEDERAL RANCH

ALASKA HIGHWAY

CAVE

INDIAN CHASE

TRUCK WRECK

SPIRIT RIVER

GOLD REEF

N

LEGEND
BOYS' ROUTE ------>
HORSES' ROUTE •••••
NOTE -- NOT DRAWN TO SCALE

chapter 1

PERRY DUG HIS BOOT HEELS INTO THE TATTERED SEAT IN
front of him as the big truck skidded dangerously on the
gravel surface of the Alaska Highway. Behind him the
horses stomped on the boards of the open truck bed. It
had been raining ever since they crossed the border south
into British Columbia and the solid gray mass of cloud
that pressed down on them showed no signs of lifting.

Perry held his breath as Joe Ferguson fought the steering wheel and brought them safely around the turn in
the road. If anybody could do it, Perry thought, it was
Joe. Perry's father and Clay's father had been buddies of
Joe's in the Korean War and they always said Joe could
do anything.

Clay, who was sitting next to Joe, turned around and
grinned at Perry. His face was reassuring. Then Tim
turned around, too. "If I were a duck," Tim said, "I'd be
happy on a day like this."

Perry felt better. As long as Tim was there to make a
joke, things couldn't be too bad. He tried to shift his
knees. Bushman, the big Irish wolfhound, was sleeping
on the seat beside him, his chin on Perry's knees. Bush-

man, who belonged to Clay, was the biggest dog Perry had ever seen.

"Hold tight," Joe said. The truck jolted as it struck a washed-out place in the road. As soon as it began, Perry knew that this skid was worse than the others. He felt the straining of the truck as Joe, almost standing, fought to straighten it out. It picked up speed and the rain, streaming through the partly opened window, struck his face. In the back the horses stamped and there was a sudden lurch as they shifted all their weight to one side.

Bushman struggled to a sitting position and whined. There was a sound of splintering wood and bending metal and then they were on their side. For a second Perry was knocked out by the jolt. When he came to, he heard moaning. Tim was doubled up in front of him.

"Tim, are you O.K.?" He bent forward anxiously.

"Yeah," Tim said. "Just shock. But Joe is hurt."

They could hear the stamping and screaming of the horses, and then the sound of hoofs galloping.

"The horses!" Clay said. "What's happening to the horses?" He pulled himself out of the cab over Tim and through the open window.

"Perry, are you O.K.?" Tim asked.

"Yes, I've got a bloody nose, that's all."

"We've got to get Joe out. I think he's hurt bad."

Perry could hear Joe moaning softly. Clay opened the cab door, reached back in, and boosted Tim out. The driving rain was pouring into the cab.

"My nose is bleeding all over the place," Perry said.

"What's your blood type?" Tim asked.

"Take it easy, you guys." Clay lifted himself through the cab door and reached for Joe. Bushman shoved past him and bounded to the ground. He disappeared at once in the dense rain.

"Is Joe conscious?" Tim asked.

"I think so," Clay said. "Joe, can you hear me?"

Joe's muffled voice reached them. "Something's busted. My leg, I think. Can you get me out of this trap?"

Tim held Clay's legs while Clay reached in for Joe. As he moved him from behind the steering wheel, Joe gasped in pain.

"Joe, I'm sorry."

"Never mind that. Just get me out of here."

Slowly, clinging to Clay's arm, Joe pulled himself up and out. By the time Clay got him out of the cab he had fainted. Perry pulled himself out just in time to help Tim and Clay lay Joe carefully on the wet ground. Clay got a poncho and put it over him.

Perry went around to the back of the truck. His nose was streaming blood. But he was thankful to be alive. With Clay and Tim and Joe, he would be all right. He checked the back of the truck. The wild horses that they had spent the last two weeks rounding up were gone, except for one. He hated to tell Joe. They were worth a hundred dollars apiece to Joe, once he got them back to Montana and broke them.

Perry saw Bushman in the rain. He whistled and the dog came loping up to him. They went back to the front of the truck. "The horses are gone," Perry said, "all except one, and he's hurt."

"Is my horse gone, too?" Joe asked, weakly.

"Yes," Perry said, "Chinook's gone."

Joe lay back on the ground. He looked discouraged.

"I'll check around," Clay said. He tilted Joe's wide-brimmed hat so it would partly protect Joe's face from the rain. He rubbed Joe's wrists. "You O.K.?"

Joe tried to move but the pain caught him again and he groaned. "Man, I'm making a lot of fuss," he said.

"Is it your leg?" Tim asked.

Cautiously Joe moved his hand over his knee. "I guess I smashed my knee. Feels like it. What a mess!"

"Are we near any town?" Clay asked. "Any place I could walk for help?"

"Let me think a minute," Joe said.

"That horse back there," Perry said. "I think his legs are broken."

"Look at him, Clay," Joe said. "You'll probably have to destroy him."

Clay reached into the upturned cab and found the 30-30 carbine. He went around to the black bulk of the overturned truck bed. Perry followed him. The truck was badly smashed. Bushman stood close to the injured horse. The horse lay on its side, heaving and groaning. Clay approached it. From the twisted position of the forelegs it was easy to see that they were broken. He lifted his gun.

"No!" Perry was shocked.

Clay looked at him.

"You can't just shoot him," Perry said.

"What do you suggest?" Usually Clay was patient, but now he sounded sharp.

"Maybe we could find a vet."

"Where do you think we are—Pasadena, California? We'll be lucky if we find a doctor for Joe." Clay lifted the gun again and aimed at the side of the horse's head. He squeezed the trigger, and the rifle cracked. The horse jerked once and lay still.

Perry turned away and bent over, being sick. He hoped Clay wouldn't notice.

In a few minutes he mopped the perspiration off his face and went back to the others. Tim had folded up one of the sleeping bags and put it under Joe's head. He was shielding the thermos of coffee so Joe could drink it.

"Never travel without coffee," Joe said. "I feel better already." He drained the thermos top he was using for a cup and gave it back to Tim. "No horses left, huh?"

"I'm sorry, Joe," Clay said.

Joe blew out his cheeks. "Well, better than a thousand bucks down the drain." He put his hands under his head. "You asked where we are. About a hundred miles from Dawson Creek."

Clay didn't answer for a moment. "Well, we can hitch

a ride. We'll find somebody to take you in."

Joe grinned. "You've got your old man's nerve. We'll just sit tight till somebody comes along. There's a good deal of traffic on this road. Somebody ought to be along pretty soon. There's a little settlement not far from here, with a Hudson's Bay Company trading post, but they wouldn't have a doctor."

"If we can get you to Dawson Creek," Clay said, "I'll stay here a bit and see if I can find those horses."

Joe thought for a minute. With his arm he wiped the rain from his face. "Well, if you'll be careful. I expect I'll be laid up a spell. We'll need to get somebody to see what can be done with the truck. How bad is it smashed?"

"Pretty bad," Clay said. "I think the rear axle is broken."

"Here's what we'll do," Joe said. "We'll make ourselves cozy here till somebody comes along. I'll pick up the first ride I can get to Dawson Creek. Then you boys walk in to Gold Reef. It's not more than an hour from here, if you short cut through the woods. But for Pete's sake be careful! If anything happens to you kids, I'll have your fathers on my neck. See what can be done about the truck. If you can find any of the horses, good, but don't be foolish. I'd like to get Chinook back if I could. Then meet me in Dawson Creek. I reckon the hospital will be a good place to look for me." He looked up at Tim. "Timmy, my lad, use that smart head of yours and fix us up some kind of shelter, you hear?"

"Oh, sure," Tim said, "like out of thin air." But he looked pleased that Joe had asked him. He scrambled back into the cab, his long legs dangling out.

"Is Perry O.K.?" Joe asked.

"Sure," said Perry. He felt faint. "I'm fine. I just got this bloody nose." He was leaning against a tree, the rain dripping off the brim of his new Stetson.

"Perry," Joe said, "what's that sign you and me was born under?"

"Pisces," Perry said.

"Well, this must be a bad day for Pisces people, that's all I got to say. You and me, we're in plumb bad luck."

"I'm sorry about your leg," Perry said. "And about

the truck. Can you fix a broken axle?"

"Not hardly," Joe said. "Not without my trusty Scout knife, and I come off without it."

"You're kidding me again," Perry said.

"Might as well kid as cry."

Tim emerged with a big tarpaulin. "If we make a kind of tent out of this tarp," he said, "we could at least get our heads out of the rain."

Deftly he attached one end of the tarp by ropes to the high end of the truck's front axle. The other end he tied to a birch tree on the grassy bank. "Now if you can ease over about a foot," he told Joe, "you'll be dry from the top anyway. I won't guarantee this house to be air-tight on the sides."

With Clay's help Joe moved a little until he was wholly under the sheltering tarp. "I knew you could do it, Timmy," he said.

"I'll get the other sleeping bags," Clay said. He rummaged around in the truck until he could reach them, and then he tossed them down to Perry. "While I'm here, here are our packs," he said, and he tossed those down, too. "We'll take them with us."

"Look at Bushman," Tim said. "He's all set." The big dog was stretched out at Joe's feet, out of the rain.

Clay unzipped Joe's sleeping bag and wrapped it around him like a blanket. Then they all curled up in their bags, as much underneath the tarp as they could get. It was cold and wet and uncomfortable, but they soon fell asleep.

When Perry awoke, the rain had cleared. There were a few rumbles of thunder off to the north, but that was all that remained of the storm. His watch read midnight, but in summer the northern nights are marked only by a slight darkening into dusk, followed in about an hour by twilight. It was light enough to read a newspaper.

Careful not to disturb the others, he crept out of his sleeping bag and stood up. Water stood in puddles everywhere and the ground was dark with it, but already it was beginning to dry out. It was cold, but it would be warm when day came.

He examined the truck carefully. It was a broken axle all right. The truck had run off the road and flipped over on its side. He looked down the road. He hoped someone would come soon. Joe needed help.

He searched for some twigs for a fire. They were wet, but he knew they were resinous enough to burn. He uncurled some loose bark from the birch to add to the fire, the way Clay had taught him. Pretty soon he had it going. There was some store-bought bread that Joe had picked up when they came through Fort Nelson. Rummaging around, Perry found some cans of beans. He got some coffee going with water from the rushing creek that flowed near the road.

Joe opened his eyes. "I smell coffee," he said, "and it's the doggone sweetest smell I ever did smell."

Bushman rolled over against Clay and woke him up.

It took some doing to get Tim awake, but soon the four of them were eating as if they had never eaten before.

Tim piled the other sleeping bags in a mound around Joe's shoulders.

"Shucks," Joe said, sipping his coffee, "if only I had me my TV set."

Perry was glad Joe felt able to joke. He sure hoped they could find some of his horses for him.

Joe had Clay get out his pocket compass and he explained to him exactly how to get to Gold Reef. The boys made sandwiches and put them in their packs. Then they sat back to wait for a car.

"You could go with Joe," Clay said to Perry, "if you'd rather not hike along with us."

Perry looked at Joe and swallowed. "I'll go along with you guys if you don't mind," he said.

Clay smiled. "Fine."

In another fifteen minutes Tim sat up straight and stared up the road. "I hear a car!"

A jeep came around the bend. The boys jumped up and waved and it slowed down and stopped. A tall, angular man climbed out from behind the wheel. "Hello," he said. "Looks like you got trouble."

Clay explained the situation to him and took him over to where Joe lay.

"If you happened to be heading for Dawson Creek . . ." Joe said.

"Well, I wasn't exactly, but I sure can," the man said.

"Haven't got room for all of you, though."

"Just Joe," Clay explained. "We're going into Gold Reef to see about getting help for the truck."

"Right you are. Then let's get this man in the jeep." Very carefully the man and the boys lifted Joe and got him into the jeep seat. Joe was deathly pale and the sweat stood out on his forehead, but he managed a grin. "O.K., you fellers, you got me off your hands now. Just take it easy and don't get lost."

"We'll wait for the truck to get fixed up and then we'll drive down to Dawson Creek," Clay said.

"All right, but take it easy."

Clay thanked the man with the jeep, and the boys stood in the road waving until the jeep and Joe were out of sight.

"All right," Clay said, "here we go."

chapter 2

FOR AWHILE THE GOING WAS EASY. THEY SOON PLUNGED into the forest, however, and without Clay's compass they would not always have been sure of the direction. In a clearing they could see the peaks of the Butler Range, running north, but once they were in the trees, in the stands of yellow poplar and blue spruce and lodgepole pine and white birch, it was not possible to see the guideline of the mountains.

Perry knew they had to move more slowly than Clay would have liked, because of him. Perry had toughened up a good deal in the ten days they had spent helping Joe with the roundup, but he was smaller than they were and not used to much exercise. He made a valiant effort to keep up, but his breath came in short gasps and he stumbled often.

Once Perry stopped and said, "Clay!"

Clay paused and looked back.

Perry was frowning. "I keep getting the feeling that something is following us."

Clay peered past him into the trees behind them. "There isn't anything there, Perry."

"Still, I got this feeling," Perry said.

"It's the ghost of the north woods," Tim said.

Perry shivered and Clay gave Tim a warning frown.

"Forget it, Perry," he said, "it's nothing except maybe a squirrel."

After a while, when Clay and Tim stopped to wait for Perry, he said, "I'm sorry. You should have left me with Joe."

"Did you want to stay with Joe?" Clay asked him.

"Heck, no! I wanted to be with you guys. It's just that I slow you down."

"It's all that athletic exercise you get, pardner," Tim said. "It cuts a man's wind."

"We'll stop a minute." Clay threw himself down on the pine needles. It felt good.

Perry looked around nervously. "Do they have bears in this part of the country?"

"Sure," Tim said. "Black bears and grizzlies. Big ones."

"We won't run into grizzly," Clay said. "Not down here."

"And Indians," Tim said. "All over. Real hostile types."

"The Indians around here are Cree and Beaver," Perry said. "I read about them. The Beaver are descended from the Sioux that came up with Sitting Bull."

"You must read a lot," Clay said.

"What else is there to do in Pasadena?" Tim asked. "Right, Perry?"

"I like to read," Perry said.

Clay got up. "You guys stay put. I want to take a look around."

"Be careful, Clay," Perry said.

"Be careful, Clay," Tim mimicked. "Wear your rubbers."

"Knock it off, Tim," Clay said. He gave Perry a quick pat on the back. "Don't worry. I'll be right back." He called Bushman and the two disappeared into the woods.

Perry wound his fingers together and studied them. "Tim," he said, "I'm sorry I slow you down and all. I probably shouldn't have come up to the north woods at all."

Embarrassed, Tim said, "Oh, forget it. I was only kidding." Busily he stuffed his pockets with twigs.

"What are you doing that for?" Perry asked. "We'll be in Gold Reef soon."

Exasperated, Tim said, "Perry, you think just like a city boy. You never know when you might need a fire. You never know about anything when you're in the wilderness. Weren't you ever a Boy Scout? 'Be prepared'!"

"My mother wouldn't let me join the Scouts," Perry said. "She thinks they do dangerous things."

Tim whistled. "How come she ever let you come up here?"

"She's in Europe. My father sent me."

There was a sudden crashing in the woods nearby. Perry shot to his feet. "Is it a bear?"

"It's probably Bushman chasing a rabbit," Tim said, but he got up, too. They stood tensely, listening. The sound died away.

"Whatever it is, it's going away," Tim said.

"Yeah," Perry said, "right in the direction we're going. Tim, what if we meet a bear?"

"Listen," Tim said, "he'll turn tail and run. Unless you happen to come between a mother and her cub."

"Then what?"

Tim shrugged. "Climb a good strong tree."

"I've never been a good climber," Perry said.

"If a bear's after you, you'll learn," Tim said.

They both wheeled around at the sound of pounding footsteps. Clay burst into the clearing with Bushman loping alongside him.

"Clay," both boys said at once, "did you hear . . ."

Clay looked triumphant. "I not only heard—I saw! It's Joe's horses! We're going to catch them."

chapter 3

"COME ON," CLAY SAID. "WE'VE GOT TO KEEP TRACK OF where they go." He was excited.

"How can we catch them?" Perry asked. He was panting as he tried to keep up with Clay.

"What if they don't go in the same direction as Gold Reef?" Tim asked.

"Then we can backtrack and follow them, after we send somebody for the truck." He looked back over his shoulder at Perry. "Even if we can only get Chinook, it'll be worth trying."

For a while it was possible to follow the trail of the horses as they ran through the woods, breaking branches and leaving footprints in the damp earth. But after a time Clay stopped. He checked his compass and shook his head. "They're veering off to the north," he said, "away from Gold Reef."

"Well, like you said, we can come back here and pick up their trail," Tim said.

"Right." Clay put his compass in his pocket and struck out in a southwesterly direction. "Joe will be laid up for a while with that knee of his so we don't have to worry about time."

"I knew a man who broke his knee and was crippled for life," Perry said.

"Well, Joe isn't going to be crippled," Clay said.

He unstrapped the little hatchet he carried attached to his belt and began making nicks in the trees as he passed them.

"Hey, are you blazing a trail?" Perry asked.

"No, he's doing a little wood carving," Tim said.

"Oh, you're so smart, Tim." But Perry didn't really mind Tim's jokes. He was getting used to the hiking now, too, and it was easier to keep up.

"Save your breath, both of you," Clay said. "We've got a way to go yet."

After a while Clay, who walked ahead of the other two, let out a yell. He pointed ahead of him. "Smoke!"

He hurried on, and the other two ran to catch up with him. They came out on a little clearing, and below them lay the tiny settlement of Gold Reef. About twenty log cabins were clustered around the Hudson's Bay Company trading post on the bank of a river.

"That's the Spirit River Joe told us about," Clay said. The river sparkled in the morning sun. Clay broke into a run, with Bushman loping along at his heels.

They were headed straight for the trading post, Clay still carrying his hatchet in his hand. As they burst into the post, dirty and disheveled, with Bushman looming beside Clay, the man behind the counter backed up and glanced toward a gun that hung on the wall.

"Hold on," the man said. "Hold it right there."

"It's O.K., mister." Clay put his hand on Bushman's collar. We've come for help." He glanced down at the hatchet in his hand and put it quickly back in the sheath.

Slowly the man relaxed. "What's the trouble?"

Clay told him what had happened.

The man grinned. "You had me fooled. I thought you was some wild customers, with that dog and all. Where in the world did you get a dog that big?"

"I got him at home in Montana," Clay said. "Is there anyone around here who could bring in the truck and fix it up?"

"Reckon I could bring it in," the man said. "My name's Hi Fuller." He and Clay shook hands. "Maybe Tom Mayberry could fix it up for you if it's not too far gone. I'll close up here and we'll go up there. You boys can come along or stay here, whichever."

"There is something we have to do," Clay said. He told him about the horses.

Mr. Fuller listened attentively. "Likely they'll head for water. From what you say, I'd expect 'em to end up in Hellgate Canyon. You can find that real easy. It's a box canyon, off to the east of the river, in between two mountains. There's a beaver meadow on the north side of it, but they most likely won't get into that 'cause there's only a narrow little opening from the canyon into the meadow. Skookum Donahue's got a trapping cabin up in that meadow, so if you got stuck overnight, you could hole up. Yes, sir, I bet you dollars to dough- nuts you'll find 'em in Hellgate Canyon."

"We'd better take some food with us," Clay said. "It might take a day or two." He looked around the Post. It was a clean, orderly place, with yard goods stacked up on counters, and guns of various kinds in racks. The place smelled of furs and guns.

While they chose the supplies he thought they would need, he described to Mr. Fuller exactly where the truck was. He spread out the supplies on the counter. A small bag of flour, a little sugar, dried apples, bacon, powdered eggs, raisins, a can of baking powder, and a frying pan.

"We can put some of this stuff in our packs," Clay said, "and then I'll pack Bushman."

"Pack a dog?" Perry said in astonishment.

"I do it all the time," Clay said. "After all, he's almost as big as a burro." He spoke to Bushman. "Up, boy." Bushman, his tongue lolling happily out of his mouth, put his huge front paws on Clay's shoulders. Clay held his hand as high as it would go, and Bushman touched it with his nose. "O.K., boy, down." Bushman dropped to the floor again and Clay patted him. Bushman gazed at him adoringly with his big amber eyes.

"That's a big dog, all right," Mr. Fuller said.

"If you've got an empty flour sack," Clay said, "I'll use it for his pack." He caught the one Mr. Fuller

tossed to him. "And if I could borrow some thread and a big needle, sir."

"Hey, you gonna sew?" Tim said, grinning.

"Sure," Clay threaded the needle that Mr. Fuller gave him. With his knife he slit the sack across the middle of one side, and sewed it together at the end. "I need something for a strap," he said.

Mr. Fuller found him a strip of old canvas, and Clay sewed it onto the sack. Then he fitted the strap over Bushman's back and the pack was secure. It made two big pockets. He filled the pockets with some of the supplies, and then tied the pack further with a narrow piece of rope.

"My gosh," Perry said, "who ever saw anything like that!"

"They don't do that in Pasadena, do they, Perry?" Tim said. "Hey, can't you see one of those chihuahuas with a back pack!" He doubled up with laughter at his own joke.

"I guess we're ready," Clay said.

"Tom and me will get your truck down here this morning," Mr. Fuller said. "If anybody can fix her up, Tom can. Now, you boys just follow the river from here and you'll come to Hellgate Canyon. It's off to the east of the river like I said, but the mountain will force you off in that direction. You can't get lost. Good luck with them horses. Use the river for your guide and stay on the east side. It's too brushy to get through on the west bank. If you find the horses took off someplace else, come on back and we'll round up some help for you."

"Thanks," Clay said. "You've sure been nice."

"Up here," Mr. Fuller said, "a man gives a hand to the next feller." He walked with them down to the river bank.

"Are there many Indians up here?" Perry asked him.

"Oh, sure. A lot of them trap. Some of 'em don't like it much that the white man's taken over their ground."

Clay adjusted his pack and helped Perry with his. Then he checked Bushman. "Bush, don't you take out after any rabbits." Bushman looked up at him. He seemed to like the pack, and to know that he was not to race around with it.

They waved goodbye to Mr. Fuller and started off down the river, away from the settlement.

"Well," Clay said, "we're on our own."

After a few minutes Perry said, "Clay, I thought I saw somebody. Just out of the corner of my eye."

"It's all those crowds of people they got out here," Tim said.

"No, really, I thought I saw a shadow."

"Maybe it's one of the people who live in Gold Reef," Clay said, "out hunting or something."

"Wouldn't he say hello?"

Clay shrugged "I didn't see anything."

"Well, maybe it was an animal. It could be an animal."

"Oh, Perry, you see things all the time," Tim said.

"I've got very sharp perceptions," Perry said.

"So sharp you see what isn't there," Tim retorted.

"It could have been a deer," Clay said.

"Or a bear," Perry said, his voice trembling a little. "It might be a bear, Clay."

Clay stopped. "Perry, look around. Do you see anything now?"

Perry peered all around. "Well, no."

"Hear anything?"

"No."

"Then let's go."

They walked in single file through the woods, but every now and then Perry glanced over his shoulder. He was sure there had been something.

chapter 4

"LET'S BREAK FOR LUNCH," CLAY SAID. THEY HAD BEEN following the broad river for a long time, and Perry was glad to stop. He was tired.

Clay chose a spot where the bank benched down to meet the water. He unloaded the pack from Bushman, who promptly flung himself into a run. He ran in tight circles around and around them, leaping bushes and dodging trees at the last moment.

Clay fished a yellow waterproofed bag out of his pack. He opened it and took out three collapsible cups and a tomato can to which a wire bail had been attached through a pair of nail holes.

"Tim," he said, "get us some birch bark, will you? Don't cut the tree. Just pull off what we need." He set to work pulling off dead spruce twigs. "These are good for starting a fire. They're full of oil."

Tim dumped out the twigs he had filled his pockets with earlier. "What'd I tell you?" he said to Perry.

"Well, there are plenty here," Perry said. "You didn't need to carry them all that way."

"You never know," Tim said.

27

"What are we going to eat?" Perry said. "I'm starved."

"You'll eat," Clay said. "Help me get that fallen poplar over here." Together they broke off the branches and dragged them to the place Clay had selected. They broke up the dry branches and Clay angled them into a wigwam shape over the birch bark and the spruce. Then he found a long green pole and shoved it in the ground at an angle. He filled the tomato can with water and hung it on the pole.

"Do you want me to light the fire?" Perry asked.

"Wait a second." Clay cut three willow wands and skewered some bacon on them.

He handed Perry one of the matches from his waterproof match case. "O.K., light it now."

With his tongue between his teeth, Perry knelt beside the pile of wood and carefully struck a match. It went out.

"Oh, boy!" Tim said.

"Strike another," Clay said, "but be careful. We don't want to waste our matches."

With fingers that trembled a little Perry tried again. This time the birch bark caught and sent up sweet black smoke. Then the spruce caught, crackling and snapping. Before it burned down into gray ash, the poplar was burning.

"O.K., cook your bacon," Clay said. "Be careful not to burn it." He showed Perry how to hold it to one side, turning it slowly.

"I'll be able to barbecue for my dad when I get home," Perry said.

Clay got out some flour, baking powder, salt, and raisins and put the ingredients together in the frying pan, adding half a cup of the stream's cold water. He worked the dough, moving quickly to prevent the leavening gas from escaping. When he had a three-inch wide dough, he wound it around a peeled stick and held it close to the fire, turning it slowly.

"What's that mess?" Perry asked.

"Listen to who's used to the Hilton Hotel," Tim said. "If Clay cooks it, it'll be good."

"It's bannock," Clay said. "Tim, dump some coffee into that boiling water."

Perry chewed thoughtfully on the broiled bacon, and then cautiously tried a piece of the steaming bannock. It came as a surprise, "Why, it's good!"

Clay grinned. "Glad you like it. Remind me to give you the recipe."

"You could sell that recipe," Perry said.

Clay laughed. "It's not mine. That's what the sour-doughs eat."

Perry was impressed. "I'm going to tell my mother about it." Then he frowned. "Although I can just see her making it for me."

"Make it yourself," Tim said. "It's no state secret."

After they had eaten, the boys rested awhile. When they were ready, they stamped out the fire and prepared to go on. Bushman was eager to be on the way. He moved around nervously while they packed up. Then he stood quietly while Clay put his pack on him.

"He likes that pack," Tim said.

As the boys were about to start on, there came a sharp cry, like an animal's cry, from nearby.

"What was that?" Perry asked. "Don't tell me I imagined that."

Clay stopped and listened. "Sounds like a coyote."

"In the middle of the day?" Tim said.

"In this country," Perry said, "how can they tell if it's day or night?"

Clay stood listening. The cry came again, from a slightly different direction.

Perry shivered. "It sounds close." He watched Clay's face. "If my dad was writing this script, that would be Indians about to attack."

"Well, this isn't TV," Clay said. "Let's go."

Perry stayed close to Clay. "It doesn't sound like a real coyote," he said.

"How would you know?" Tim said. "They got coyotes in Pasadena?"

"No," Perry said, "of course not, but I visited my aunt in San Marcos and they got coyotes up in the hills. They used to howl every night. They sounded different."

"Your coyotes had a southern accent," Tim said.

They followed the river as it wound through the woods. Then they came to the mountain. It was impossible now to stay with the river. A faint game trail led alongside a small tributary stream that wound eastward.

"Here's where we head east for the canyon," Clay said. The little stream was not more than three feet wide although in places it ran two feet deep. They struck off in that direction.

"I'll bet Mr. Fuller was right," Tim said. "Bet those old horses headed right for that box canyon."

"You're just surmising," Perry said.

Tim grinned. "I surmise all the time."

The sun was high in the sky and the air was warm. The stream clattered along in some places and then slowed down to a quiet trickle. They followed it for quite a while. Then Clay, who was in front, broke into a trot. In a minute he called back, "Here it is."

The boys caught up with him as he stood at the entrance to the box canyon. The stream was very narrow here and it flowed sluggishly over the grassy floor of the canyon.

At the far end of the canyon, horses were grazing.

chapter 5

"Look," Clay said, "there's Joe's horse, Chinook. She's still got her halter on."

"Good," Tim said. "We can use her to round up the others."

"It shouldn't be too hard in this canyon," said Clay. "I wish we had some rope. Why didn't I think to bring some rope!"

"How are we going to catch them?" Perry asked.

"I got to think about it awhile," Clay said.

"Maybe they'll run away while you're thinking."

"No, there's no place they can go except back up the canyon past us."

Leading the way, Clay slid down a short embankment into the canyon. "You guys stay here. I want to see if I can get Chinook. If the horses start back this way, don't let them get past you."

"How do we stop them?" Perry asked.

"Yell. Flap your arms. Shoo them like hens."

"Oh, great," Perry said. "So now we're horse shooers."

Tim yelled with laughter. "Hey, old Perry made a joke."

Clay studied the end of the canyon. "First, though, I think I'll take a look at the other end of the canyon."

"Can I come with you?" Perry asked. He liked to go with Clay. Exciting things happened.

"Sure," said Clay.

They walked slowly down the canyon. Its sides rose up steeply from the floor. They were made of loose shale. It would be impossible to climb them. Beyond, the mountains reared up on both sides.

They went on to the end. There was a narrow, almost invisible opening, as Mr. Fuller had said, just wide enough for one horse to get through. It was partly hidden by overgrowing brush. Clay found the opening and stepped through. He held the bushes back for Perry. On the other side there was the beaver meadow, widening out on both sides.

"Mr. Fuller mentioned a trapper's cabin," Clay said. "It might have some rope in it." He started across the meadow.

There was an abundance of vetch, good grazing for the horses if they only knew it was there. Off to the West there was a big blueberry patch.

"Hey," Perry said, "can we get some berries?"

"On the way back," Clay said. He studied the berry patch. "A good place to find bear," he added with a grin, "if you want a bear."

Perry shivered. "I'm scared of bear."

"They won't hurt you," Clay said, "unless you happen to get between a mother and her cub. Or unless you bother them, of course." He shaded his eyes and looked around the meadow. There was no cabin in sight. "Let's go a little farther."

It was pleasant walking in the meadow. As they skirted the berry patch, both boys scooped up a handful of berries. "Look," Clay said, "there's a bear sign." He pointed to places where great swipes of a bear's paws had broken off the bushes.

At the far edge of the meadow a line of willow trees marked the spot where the woods began again. "A cabin would be inside the line of trees," Clay said.

The sun shone warmly on their shoulders. Perry wished he had left his jacket behind. He took it off and tied the sleeves around his waist.

In a few minutes they came to the willows, and there was the cabin, a small but sturdily built structure. Eagerly they went toward it. The slab door was unlocked. They pushed it open and went in. The clean, resin-yellowed walls were chinked with sphagnum moss. There was a moosehide chair wired up out of reach of pack rats and squirrels. In one corner there was a small cookstove. Slab shelves rested on pegs. The woods smelled of a tarry preservative. In another corner, also secured out of reach of sharp-toothed animals, was the rope Clay had hoped to find, and on the floor below it was a roll of snare wire.

Clay got the rope down. "Not as much as I wish there

was, but it will do," he said.

"Can we just take it?" Perry asked.

"We'll arrange to replace it when we get back to town. If we go on after the other horses, there may be another cabin. Trappers usually build a series of cabins in a circle about seven or eight miles apart over the area of their traplines." Clay looped the rope over his shoulder. "Let's go back."

When they came to the blueberries again, they stopped to pick some. They filled their pockets and Perry made a basket out of his jacket. Suddenly Clay touched his arm. "Look," he said quietly.

Perry looked up. "My gosh," he said, "aren't they cute!" Two fat brown bear cubs were rolling over each other, not far from where they stood. Then he said quickly, "Where's the mother?"

"Yeah," Clay said. "Where?" He looked around.

Perry's heart began to pound. "Are they grizzlies?"

"I think they're black bear, but I'm not sure." Cautiously he looked over his shoulder. Perry saw his face change. Hastily Perry threw a frightened glance behind him. His stomach turned cold. A big bear was lumbering toward them. She came at a half run, awkward and swaying. There were no trees near by that were big enough to climb. The blueberries in Perry's clenched hand ran blue juice down his fingers. He was unaware of them. He was conscious only of the advancing bear. The cubs sat up for a moment and looked at her, then went back to their playing. The mother bear would have to pass within a few yards of the boys to reach the cubs.

"What are we going to do?" Perry's voice shook.

"Just stand absolutely still," Clay said. "Don't move, no matter what happens."

Keeping himself from running was the hardest thing Perry had ever done, but he did as Clay said.

As the bear came closer, Clay began to talk to her in a low, soothing voice. "O.K., bear, we aren't going to hurt your babies. Just take it easy, bear. Nobody is going to hurt them. Just take it easy, now, old mama bear."

When she was about fifty yards from them the bear stopped and glared at them with her tiny eyes. Her head swayed back and forth. One of the cubs howled, and the bear shifted her gaze toward him. Then she looked back at Clay and Perry. The two cubs started to play again, growling and scuffling. The bear came closer and closer in her direct approach to the cubs. When she was forty feet from them, she sidled sideways past them, keeping her eyes fixed on them. Finally she reached the cubs and touched each of them with her nose. Then she waddled off in the opposite direction, the cubs following her. In a moment they stopped to play and she came back, the impatient mother, to nudge them on their way. She spanked them with her huge paw and they scampered along obediently. The two boys stood completely still until finally the bears disappeared in the woods. Then with a shaky sigh of relief, Clay said, "Well, how did you like that?"

Perry took a long, quivering breath. "I never thought I'd live through it."

chapter 6

WHEN THEY GOT BACK INTO THE CANYON, PERRY MOVED down toward Tim while Clay went to get Chinook.

She was off by herself, grazing, a big horse, compared to the small Alaskan horses. Her shiny black coat glistened in the sun. She had been cut on the flank in the accident. Perry watched Clay as he came up to her slowly, holding out a handful of vetch.

"Chinook . . . Hey, Chinook." He spoke softly and reassuringly. "Come on, girl, don't be frightened. Easy, girl."

She tossed her head and whinnied.

"Easy, girl, easy."

She danced a little away from him. The other horses looked over at them, watching him tensely. He stood still, not wanting to spook them. Only when they settled down did he move the hand that held the vetch again and take a careful step forward.

"Here you are, girl."

This time she stood still and let him approach her. He reached out slowly and, giving her the vetch with one hand, took hold of her bridle with the other. Now it was safe to come close, rub her head, and scratch her ears.

"Good girl. Good old Chinook. Come on, girl. Let's go." He led her back to Tim and Perry, who had watched it all closely. Bushman bounded over and ran a few circles of welcome around Chinook. Chinook let fly with a hoof and Bushman ducked and loped and circled, in the old familiar game.

"How are we going to catch the other horses?" Tim asked. "What's the plan?"

"I'll ride Chinook," Clay said, "and see if I can rope them. You and Perry keep them from running back down the canyon. Tim, if you'll stay here, then Perry down there by the entrance to the canyon. Just like I said, flap your arms and jump up and down and yell if they ease toward you. You know, Perry, you've seen how Joe does."

"O.K.," Perry said, but he felt doubtful.

Clay mounted Chinook and slung the rope in loose coils around his arm.

"Make Bush stay with you. Hang onto his collar if you have to. He'll just get in my way. Stay, Bushman! Stay, boy."

Perry went to his station and watched Clay as he rode toward the nearest horse. The horse lifted his head as they approached, and then with a ducking motion he began to weave away from Clay. But Clay was a good hand with a horse, and Chinook was a cutting horse.

Clay managed in just a few minutes to back the horse up against the side of the canyon and to rope him. He jumped down off Chinook and ran toward the little horse, taking up the slack on the rope as the horse reared and ducked from one side to the other. When Clay had him under control, he made a hackamore of the rope and led him to Tim.

He cut a length of the rope, leaving enough for a hackamore, and turned the horse over to Tim. "Remind me to buy some new rope for Mr. Fuller to give to that trapper," he said. "Now hang onto this boy."

He caught the next two horses in the same way, but the fifth one was wary. She managed to elude Clay's rope and to race past Chinook. Perry saw her coming straight for him. He was frightened. But Clay had said to yell and jump, so he yelled and jumped for all he was worth.

Startled, the mare came to a sliding stop. She tried to duck around Perry, but each time he anticipated her. They were still matching wits when Clay reached them. He threw the rope neatly over the horse's head. In a flash Clay was on the ground fighting the game little mare. She was harder to subdue than the others. Clay was swung off his feet and almost thrown to the ground, but he recovered his balance and fought the horse to a standstill.

"O.K., little girl," he said, panting and trying to pat her neck, "you're a tough little horse. Now just cool off." And to Perry he said, "You did a good job."

Clay's praise made Perry feel good.

When the mare had quieted a little, Clay led her back and with Tim's help he roped the five horses together and tied them securely to pines that grew near the sides of the canyon.

"Whew!" Clay said. "Well, we made it."

"That was good work, Clay," Tim said.

"I couldn't have done it alone," Clay said.

"Hey, old Perry boy," Tim said, "that was a nice piece of whoopin' and hollerin' you did there. I was proud of you."

"You don't have to make fun of everything," Perry said.

"Who's making fun? I mean it. It's scary when a horse comes charging at you."

Mollified, Perry said, "Well, thanks. I ride some at the North Hollywood stables."

"Eastern?" Tim said.

"Sure."

Tim grinned but he said nothing.

"Look at Chinook," Clay said. "She doesn't like those wild cayuses one little bit." The black mare was standing with her back to the four wild horses, her head averted. "A real snob horse."

"Hey," Tim said, "I'm hungry."

"Let's go to that cabin," Perry said.

Clay shook his head. "We'll bed down here. I don't want to risk moving the horses around more than we have to. It's kind of tricky through that opening into the meadow, especially if they're roped together." He got up. "We'll eat and sleep here and get an early start back. If you and Tim will get the fire going, I'll fix us a bed."

With his hatchet he cut spruce boughs and thatched them into a bed big enough for the three of them. By the time he had finished, the boys had the fire going. Clay made some more bannock, and got out the powdered eggs and scrambled some in the frying pan. Tim and Perry cooked bacon and coffee again. They ate every bit, and when the coffee was gone, they unpacked the powdered milk and mixed it with cold water from their canteens. The blueberries made a welcome dessert, even though they were somewhat squashed.

It was only five o'clock, but they decided to sleep awhile before they started back to the settlement. Clay checked the horses once more and then lay down. In a few minutes all three of them and Bushman were sound asleep.

chapter 7

IT WAS JUST PAST THE HALF DARK OF TWILIGHT AND starting to lighten again when Bushman sat up and barked. His deep, strong voice brought the boys awake. Tim turned over and went back to sleep. Clay looked around, half awake, and said, "Quiet, Bush." Perry sat up.

"What is it, Clay?" he asked.

"He probably heard a porcupine or something," Clay said. "Go to sleep."

But Perry couldn't sleep. The idea of a porcupine did not make him happy. Shivering a little, he hunched up his knees and sat staring across the canyon. He could hear coyotes barking, and this time they sounded like the coyotes of San Marcos. And far away, almost beyond hearing, he detected a howl. Wolves, he thought—timber wolves. For a minute he wished he were home in Pasadena, but then he reminded himself that he had to be grown-up like Clay. "Be a man," his father had told him. "Toughen up, son." Well, he was doing his best. Even Tim had said he did a good job of shooing the horse. He had not run when the little mare came at him, although he had felt like it. And he had not run away from the bear. Being brave, his father had told him, doesn't mean never being scared—anyone in his right mind gets scared sometimes. Being brave means not giving way to panic. And he hadn't given way.

Bushman was still sitting up. He leaned over now and pushed his cold nose against Perry's neck. "Hey," Perry said softly, "cut that out."

Bored with sleep, Bushman nuzzled him again. This time the push was so strong it almost toppled Perry over.

"Oh, O.K.," Perry said. "I'll go for a little walk with you, but just a little one. I want some more sleep." He got to his feet and started up the canyon.

With Bushman jogging happily ahead of him, he picked his way along the floor. Above him the mountain peaks in the dim light seemed eerie and unreal.

He wandered on until Bushman stopped so suddenly that Perry almost fell over him.

"What's the matter?" Perry demanded. Then he put his hand over his mouth. Clearly imprinted in the damp earth was a gigantic print of what looked like some tremendous prehistoric bird or perhaps, Perry thought, a dinosaur. He had never seen anything like it. He could not imagine what could have made such a print. He opened his mouth to call to Clay, but first he glanced over to the place where the horses had been tied. They were gone. Every one of them, even Chinook, had disappeared. There was not even a dangling end of rope to show that they had ever been there.

"Clay!" Perry yelled as loud as he could, and he turned, half stumbling over Bushman, and ran back to the sleeping boys. "Clay! Clay! The horses are gone. There's a monster!"

chapter 8

CLAY WAS ON HIS FEET AT ONCE AND RUNNING DOWN THE
edge of the river behind Perry.

"Look!" Perry said. "It's a monster."

Clay stared at the print in disbelief. "What *is* it? I
never saw anything like it."

"It looks like a pterodactyl or something," Perry said,
his voice trembling.

Tim came up behind them, rubbing his eyes. "Good
grief! What's that?"

"The horses are gone." Clay sounded discouraged.
"There's not a sign of them."

"But that print, Clay," Tim said soberly. "It must be
five feet across. What makes a track like that?"

"Nothing," Perry said. "Nothing real. It has to be a
prehistoric monster or something."

"A bird monster," Tim said.

"My mother believes in psychic phenomena," Perry
said. "Not that I do. But she does. Like poltergeists and
things."

"What's a poltergeist?" Tim asked.

"Oh, never mind that nonsense," Clay said. "Let's find

out what's happened to those darned horses." He went
to the trees where they had been tied. "Not a sign of a
rope." He looked around on the ground, puzzled. "If
they broke loose, they'd have left some rope."

"Maybe you just didn't tie it tight enough," Tim said.

"I was very careful about tying them. Look, the tracks
go across the canyon." He followed the prints to the
edge of the little stream. They reappeared on the other
side.

Perry and Tim followed him. Bushman circled the
tracks, sniffing. The boys set off at a fast walk, heading
toward the north end of the canyon. When they got
there, Clay stopped and shook his head. "It doesn't make
sense."

"What doesn't?"

"They found that opening and went through it, one
by one. How could they? You can't even see the opening unless you push back the brush. Horses aren't that
smart." He looked up at the heavy rocks at the top of
the narrow precipice.

"The ghost took them through," Tim said, grinning.

Clay pushed aside the wolf willow that grew over the
opening and stepped through. "They're in the meadow,"
he called back.

Tim and Perry followed him into the meadow. There,
at the far end, were the horses.

"We'll never catch them in here," Tim said. "Especially without a rope."

"Why don't we just go home, Clay?" Perry asked.

"I can at least get Chinook," Clay said. "And maybe we can find the rope. It has to be somewhere."

"Clay, you can't catch those horses in an open meadow," Tim said.

"We could make a fence," Clay said. "There's snare wire in the cabin. Let's get our gear and put it in the cabin. We'll make us a fence." He started back to the canyon.

When they had moved all their gear to the cabin, Clay explained to them how he intended to make a fence out of notched poles and wire. He took his hatchet out of the sheath. "You guys help me find the right kind of branches."

"Where do we put this fence?" Tim asked.

"Down there by the clump of poplars. We'll drive some posts into the ground right at the edge of the meadow. Then when it's done, I'll ride Chinook and herd them into it. I think we can do it."

For several hours the three boys worked hard, chopping thick branches, pounding posts into the soft earth, cutting V's in the uprights. Finally they had a crude series of notched poles set up for a fence. To these Clay added heavy branches, which he wired to the two sides of the fence.

"Now to get Chinook."

"Gosh, let's eat first," Tim said.

They went back to the cabin and ate some raisins and

some dried apples.

"We can't stay after today," Clay said. "We're almost out of food."

Perry looked around. "I read a book once about living off the country. There's a lot of stuff around here we could eat if we had to. But we won't have to," he added quickly.

Clay stretched out for a few minutes on the rough floor of the cabin. "If we get the horses rounded up, we'll start right back," he said. "But we've got to find that rope. I don't know how I happened to come off without rope. That was a dumb tenderfoot thing to do."

"You said it, I didn't," Tim chimed in.

"Well, you had a lot on your mind," Perry said. "Besides, if you had had your own rope, it would be lost now."

"I just can't figure out how they got in here," Clay said.

"I could look for the rope," Perry said. "It has to be somewhere. At least I think it does."

"O.K.," Clay said. "You might look around for it, Perry. We sure need it."

"First I'll help you with the horses. Bushman and I can stay down here near the corral."

"All right, let's go." Clay got up.

Perry set off across the meadow, his hand on Bushman's collar. Clay and Tim angled off to the end of the meadow where the horses were. Chinook was grazing a little apart from the others. Clay walked up to her. She lifted her head and watched him, but this time she made no move to elude him. In a minute he was on her back.

Once that was accomplished, Tim came running down to help Perry at the corral. When the boys were set, Clay began the job of cutting out the horses and driving them one by one into the enclosure. The first one went in almost at once. When he found himself trapped, he reared and plunged at the fence, but Tim and Perry yelled and waved their hats and kept him away from the opening.

The other horses were harder to catch, and it took Clay time and some tricky riding before he managed at

last to drive them all into the little corral. But at last he dismounted in a leap and helped Tim secure the gate.

"Old Chinook is a darned good cutting horse," he said. "She did a fine job. Now if that fence is only high enough so they won't jump it."

"It ought to do for a while." Tim said.

"Let's get back to the cabin. I'm bushed."

But Perry took Bushman and walked along the edge of the meadow. All at once he caught sight of something. He could hardly believe his eyes. He picked it up carefully and ran back to Clay and Tim.

"But look at it," Perry said. "That's just how I found it."

"What do you mean?"

"See how it's coiled? I found it like that. All neat and coiled up like that."

"Oh, you're exaggerating," Tim said.

"I am not. I carried it back just the way I found it, to show you guys. And you can tell me, maybe, how it got like that. No horse ever coiled a rope."

The boys stared at the rope as Perry laid it neatly on the ground.

"How could it happen?" Clay said.

"There's something eerie in these woods," Perry said. "Clay, let's go home."

chapter 9

CLAY SAT CROSS-LEGGED ON THE GROUND IN FRONT OF THE cabin and faced the other boys. "Listen," he said, "I don't know the answer to all these things, but there has to *be* an answer. There's an answer for everything. Like maybe the rope just happened to fall like that. It's unusual, but I guess it could happen."

"Oh, come on, Clay," Perry said, "a long rope just doesn't happen to fall in a perfect coil."

"But it was there," Clay said. "It got there somehow, and there are no such things as ghosts or monsters."

"It was funny, though," Tim said. "And that footprint and all."

"It probably wasn't a track at all," Clay said. "Maybe some branches fell or . . ." He trailed off as his own explanation struck him as inadequate. "Anyway," he went on briskly, "we have the horses and we have the rope. We'll start back as soon as we've had a little sleep. I'll fix some bannock and coffee and we'll sleep. Then we'll be on our way. So cheer up, Perry."

"I'll get some blueberries," Tim said.

"All right, but keep your eyes open. Take Bushman

along with you."

Tim and Bushman set off for the blueberry patch.

Clay sat for a moment staring out across the meadow at the horses. He frowned thoughtfully. Then he shook his head and got up.

"Help me get wood for a fire," he said.

When it was ready, Tim still had not returned so Clay set about making another browse bed. He gathered springy evergreen boughs. Cutting and staking four poles in the shape of a big bed, he laid small spruce branches at the head. He put the branches with the under sides up and the butts pointing toward the foot. Row after row were laid closely together until the mattress was about a foot thick. Then Clay made it level with soft evergreen tips shoved in wherever there was space. Perry tried it. It was springy and comfortable. He wondered if he could do it himself.

As he saw Tim start back toward the cabin, Clay carefully struck one of his precious matches and got the fire going. He filled the tomato can with water from the stream and set it to boil.

Tim was in high spirits. He had not only been picking, but eating, and he had telltale blue smears on his hands and face.

"Boy, are they good!" Perry said, helping himself.

"I'm glad you left a few," Clay said.

They sat down in the green kinnikinnic that covered the ground and ate their bannock and blueberries and drank their coffee.

"My mother doesn't let me drink coffee at home," Perry said, looking at his cup with satisfaction. "It's good, isn't it?"

"It'll make a man of you, Perry, my boy," Tim said. "I've been drinking it since I was a lad, and look at me." He grinned at Perry.

"If *that's* what it leads to . . ." Perry said, and he pretended to dump his cup. He liked it when Tim kidded him. It made him feel as if he belonged.

"Let's clean up and turn in," Clay said. "All the trouble I went to with this bed, you better make the most of it."

It was a little after midnight when a noise awoke them. It sounded, Perry thought afterwards, like Niagara Falls. The three of them sat up almost at once. Clay got to his knees, straining to see the corral.

"The horses!" He leaped up, and without stopping to put on his boots he raced to the corral. Already three of the horses were gone, and he was just in time to stop Chinook and one roan stallion. Tim and Perry, coming close behind him, helped him drive the two horses back. Then they reached to put the gate in place.

Clay stopped and frowned. "Look at this."

"What?"

"They didn't knock the gate down. The wire has been unwound. Here it is on the ground."

"What's going on here?" Tim sounded scared.

Together they put the gate back into place. The escaped horses were out of sight.

"We'll take Chinook and the stallion and go back," Clay said. "Right now. I've had it."

Perry went ahead of them to round up Bushman. When he came to the passage into the canyon he stared in disbelief. He ran as hard as he could back to the cabin.

"Clay! Tim! There's been an avalanche. The pass to the canyon is blocked. That was the noise that woke us up."

Clay looked for a long moment. Then he sat down heavily. "We're cut off," he said.

chapter 10

THE OTHER BOYS STARED AT CLAY IN DISMAY.

"Well," Clay said finally, "we'll have to circle around through the forest until we can get back to the river. As soon as we get beyond those mountains, we can work our way back to the river. It'll take us longer, but we can do it."

"How do we get upstream, past the mountains, then?"

"We'll go up the other side of the river."

"We're almost out of grub," Tim said.

"With any luck we can get some small game. We'll manage. Now why don't you guys get another couple hours of sleep, and I'll stay here and watch the horses."

Perry shuddered. "I can't sleep."

"Of course you can," Clay said, a little abruptly.

"This wilderness is scary," Perry said. "I want to get out of here." His voice broke. "I want to go home."

"Perry," Clay said patiently, "we all want to go home. We're going, just as fast as we can. But now you need some sleep. There's a long hike ahead of us."

"Come on, Perry," Tim said.

"I think I'll stay here and help Clay," Perry said.

Tim shrugged and went back to the cabin. Clay and Perry made themselves as comfortable as possible, sitting with their backs against the posts of the corral. Chinook came and hung her head over the gate.

"Well," Clay said, reaching up and rubbing the horse's velvety nose, "there are a bunch of questions that are hard to answer, but there's a good answer to them somewhere. Everything has an answer."

"What do you really think it is, Clay?" Perry asked.

Clay sighed. "I don't know. Maybe some mean trapper —I don't know. There are all kinds of people even in the wilderness."

"But that track," Perry said. "Isn't it some kind of animal?"

"What animal makes a track like that?" Clay straightened his back. Deep in the woods behind them an owl hooted, and far away they heard the minor song of a wolf.

"We'll have to find some meat," Clay said. "Maybe I can get a rabbit."

"That would be good."

"They're O.K., but not for long."

"Why not?"

"You get rabbit fever. Protein poisoning. You need meat with fat on it. Bear is the best. But we can't get big game without a gun, of course. Porcupine would be good."

"Porcupine!" Perry was horrified.

"Very tasty. My dad told me almost anything is O.K. if you cook it slow and easy. He's even eaten mud hen, but he stuffed it with wild onions, and we don't have any onions. An unstuffed hen would taste like an old moccasin, I guess. Well, one way or another, we'll make out all right." He got out his compass and began drawing a map in the dirt.

"What do you think caused that avalanche?" Perry asked.

Clay was a long time in answering. "It seems like somebody got it going," he said, "but I don't know."

chapter 11

PERRY SHIVERED. THE NIGHTS WERE COOL AND HE WISHED they had brought their sleeping bags. For just the couple of nights they planned to be gone, they'd thought they wouldn't need them.

Inside the corral the stallion moved restlessly. Once he reared and struck out with his front feet at the poles of the fence.

"O.K.," Clay said, "we'll both warm up." He called Chinook to the gate, opened the gate part way, and mounted her. He dropped the rope over the stallion's head. The horse bucked and reared, but Clay got him out of the corral and into a wide smooth place in the meadow. He took with him one of the thinned spruces from the corral, and, sliding off Chinook, he pounded it into the ground with his hatchet handle. Then he looped an end of the rope around it. "All right, horse," he said. "We've got a snubbing post. Let's wear off some of that energy."

Perry watched, fascinated. The stallion ran hard at the taut end of the rope, around and around in a big circle. Clay let him run for a long time, until at last the fight began to go out of him. Clay then called to Perry, and riding Chinook and leading the tired stallion, he headed for the cabin. He tied both horses securely to a couple of pines and went inside to wake Tim. It was time to be on their way.

When they had finished their meager breakfast, Tim and Perry mounted Chinook's broad back and Clay led the stallion. Clay walked ahead. He had planned a route that led through the forest and circled around until it came back to the river.

As soon as they were well inside the forest, it was no longer possible to see the mountains for a guide, so Clay checked the compass often. It was pleasant in the woods. The morning sun filtered down through the trees and made patterns of light on the forest floor. Chipmunks chirped and squirrels chattered and scolded them as they passed. "If necessary," Clay said, "we could eat squirrel."

Perry hated the idea, but decided if it was necessary they could.

They came upon a clearing after awhile and Bushman took out after a rabbit.

"Stay here a minute," Clay said. "I may be able to get us some lunch." He followed Bushman across the opening. He could see the hare now and then. It was circling to avoid Bushman, so he crouched in the fragrant grass and waited. Sure enough, it came hopping back in great leaps. It stopped for a moment, only its ears showing. Clay tensed and then jumped. The hare lay still, his neck

broken by the weight of Clay's body. Clay pushed the
eager Bushman aside.

The boys built a fire and Clay cooked the rabbit.

"It's like chicken, only better," Perry said. He leaned
back contentedly.

They started out again, this time Clay and Perry
riding and Tim walking. It seemed to Perry that they
were making good time but it was hard to tell. He hoped
it would be this easy all the way.

A long time later they came to the river. Clay was
jubilant. "Bless the old compass," he said.

"Yeah," Tim said, "But tell me how we're going to

get upstream."

The terrain directly below them rose sharply into mountainous land. As far as they could see downstream, there were mountains.

"We'll have to try the other side," Clay said. "It's important to keep the river for our guide."

The river was swift here. Clay led the stallion across the stream. The horse fought him all the way. Clay was drenched by the time he got him across. Chinook went calmly, led by Tim. Perry splashed across, holding up the last of their supplies. Once they were all on the other side, they looked around. It was not much more promising than the side they had just left. The land rose and dipped sharply; it was covered with gravelly and thick brush.

"We'll never get the horses through all that," Tim said.

"Sure we can," Clay said, but he did not sound altogether convinced.

Tim's mouth set in a straight line. "Show me," he said. He sat down on the ground.

Clay took the stallion by the halter and started up the first of the slopes. He fought the brush, trying to lead the horse in the smoothest way. But there was no smooth way. The stallion fought every inch, and when the gravel slipped under his hooves, he neighed sharply and pulled free from Clay's hand. Tim jumped up and caught him as he came plunging down the slope, eyes wild with fear.

Clay slid back down. "You're right," he said. "We can't make it that way."

"We'll have to strike into the forest," Tim said, "and then circle around back toward Gold Reef."

"I don't like it," Clay said, "but I guess you're right."

They got up and walked into the forest. The dimness and quiet enveloped them at once.

They walked in silence for a long time, Clay checking the compass often. After what seemed to Perry like hours, Tim called back, "There's a pond or something up ahead."

Clay nudged Chinook to hurry her up.

It was not a pond; it was a good-sized lake, a beautiful one with woods growing right down to the shore. "Animals must come here to drink," Clay said. "At least it's a good place for game."

He got off the mare and went down to the shore, trying to figure which would be the easiest way around it. It stretched out of sight in both directions.

"Let's look around," he said. The boys set out along the shore to the West, hoping to be able to see the end of the lake when they rounded the bend. They found that they could not see it, so they went back in the other direction. Here they could see that the lake narrowed to what looked like an end, although they couldn't be sure it didn't just extend around a curve of the shoreline. Clay stood there indecisively. Then his eye caught something bobbing gently near the shore. He went closer.

It was an old rowboat, secured by a chain to an over-hanging willow. Clay let out a shout.

"Look," he said, "a boat. And somebody has used it since the ice went out of the lake."

"Maybe there's a cabin," Tim said.

"If we're lucky, we'll find another trapping cabin," Clay said. "Let's look." They tied the horses to trees and spread out in the general area of the boat.

After a little while Perry called, "I've found it!"

He burst out of the trees, excited and proud at his discovery. "Look, it's a beautiful little cabin."

It was slightly bigger than the one they had found in the meadow, and there were more things in it. Clay pointed to the ceiling, where equipment had been tied up. "A fishing pole! Hey, we'll have trout for supper."

There were pots and pans, a coil of rope, and two chairs made out of birch branches and rope.

"We can stay here tonight," Clay said.

"I wish this was a vacation," Tim said. "We could stay here awhile. This is really neat. Hey, Clay, I'm going fishing."

"There are some fish hooks and line here," Clay said, exploring further. "Bring us back some whoppers, Timmy."

"What are you going to do?" Tim asked.

"I'm going to take the stallion back to the clearing and work him out. Maybe I can get him half broke before we get back. Anyway, he'll be easier to travel."

Tim unfastened the pair of oars, while Perry attached hook and line to the pole for him. "My dad would flip if he saw this," Perry said. "He paid thirty-five dollars for his fishing rod."

"The fish don't know the difference," Tim said.

He was already out on the lake by the time Clay and Perry and Bushman had set out for the clearing with the stallion.

chapter 12

PERRY SAT COMFORTABLY ON A STUMP IN THE SUN, holding Chinook's rope while she grazed.

The little stallion was learning fast. After Clay had worked with him awhile, he no longer fought the rope. He seemed almost to enjoy the game of racing around the snubbing post that Clay had pounded into the middle of the clearing. After a while he let Clay approach him. Though he stood tensely while Clay patted his neck and talked to him, he made no attempt to shy off or to rear as he had done at first.

"You're coming along real good, little horse," Clay told him. "We'll have you part broke before we get back to Joe."

He untied the rope from the snubbing post. "Let's go," he said to Perry. He looked around him. "Let's circle around a little, to see what the country is like." After a while he stopped. "Listen. It sounds like a big animal thrashing around."

Perry grew pale. Perhaps it was whatever had been following them.

"Maybe it's a moose," Clay said. "I wish I had a gun."

They went through a stand of lodgepole pine. Off to the East the land tilted sharply and water trickled down over the rocks of the incline. They kept on, following the sound. They heard an animal's cry. "If I didn't know better," Clay said, "I'd swear that was a horse." He jumped over a downfall of branches. The trees thinned.

Suddenly the stallion, who was slightly ahead of him, pulled back so sharply that he almost stepped on Perry. Bushman swerved around him, and then he, too, stopped short and jerked back. His front feet had sunk down. Clay grabbed his collar and pulled him back.

"Hold it," Clay said. "It's muskeg."

"What's that?" Perry felt the ground quaking under him.

"A peat bog in the making."

Clay moved cautiously to the left, in the direction of the sound he had heard. The stallion pulled on the rope, but Clay paid out the rope as far as it would go and pulled on it. "It might be a moose," he said. "Only moose, with their wide-spreading hooves, can usually navigate a bog like this." He pushed aside the branches of a birch tree and there, only a few feet from them, was a horse, mired down in the bog. She had sunk to her shoulders.

Clay took a quick look. "Wait here," he said. He ran as fast as he could back through the woods, the stallion flying along behind him. In a few minutes he was back, riding Chinook and carrying a rope. Perry had been watching the trapped horse anxiously. It had given up struggling. Clay dropped the rope over her shoulders. He tried to pull, but he got nowhere.

"I'll try a tail hitch," he said. He made a half hitch high up on Chinook's tail, then bent the tail back on itself, and tied a second half hitch over the doubled tail.

"I've used this method with my own horse when I brought in loads of firewood at home—small trees and heavy logs," he said.

He moved Chinook a little to the left until he could pull the mired horse backwards.

"Her neck will break," Perry said.

"Let's hope not."

The horse began to move as Chinook pulled. Then, with a great sucking noise, it came straight back, and the next moment it lay on its side. It struggled up and scrambled to solid ground. It stood there, covered with mud, soaking wet and shivering. It was the little mare that had given Clay so much trouble in the canyon. She was in no mood for trouble now. She stood meekly while Clay rubbed her wet sides.

"Come on, girl," he said, "we'll get you back to the cabin and rub you down."

She followed the boys quietly back to the cabin. Clay found an old burlap bag and Perry rubbed her down.

By the time he had finished, the boat was heading in toward shore. Tim yelled and waved and held up his hands to indicate a big fish.

Clay and Perry went down to the shore to meet him. As the boat nosed ashore, Tim handed over the fish to Perry. Perry gave it to Clay and jumped into the water to get the bow of the boat. He tripped over the root of a pine tree and fell headlong. Tim whooped with laughter. But Perry did not get up. He half sat up and turned his face toward Clay. It was white and strained with pain.

"I did something to my ankle," he said apologetically.

"Let me look," Clay said. He touched the ankle gently. Perry winced. The ankle had already begun to swell. "I can't tell whether it's broken or sprained," Clay said, "but it doesn't look very good." He looked at Perry's averted face. "Gee, I'm sorry, Perry."

There were tears in Perry's voice. "I spoil everything. Now I've really wrecked things."

"Listen," Clay said, "if somebody had to be laid up for a day or so, it couldn't have happened at a better place. We've got a good cabin, a lake full of fish, a watering place to find game, three horses, and right over behind the cabin, a patch of cranberries. So cheer up!"

"Sure," Tim said. "We got it made. I wanted to stay here awhile anyway. We'll have a good vacation. Clay and I'll make you a splint for your ankle, Perry, and some crutches and all. You'll get around as good as new."

Perry looked from Tim to Clay. He knew he had tears in his eyes. "You guys are real good guys," he said. "So O.K., where's that splint?"

chapter 13

CLAY AND TIM CARRIED PERRY TO THE CABIN AND MADE him as comfortable as possible. He sat in one of the birch chairs and rested his foot on the other. Tim got cold water from the lake and made cold compresses for the badly swollen ankle.

"I never can remember whether it should be hot compresses or cold compresses," he said. "I hope it's cold."

"We'd better heat some water and alternate them," Clay said. "I think that's what you're supposed to do." Swiftly he got a fire going in the cabin's stove, which was a big steel drum. "There's a chill in the air anyway. It won't hurt to keep a fire going."

He had some aspirin in his pack, and he gave some to Perry. Then he went outside and cut some wood for a splint.

"If I didn't know it was July," Tim said, "I'd say it was going to snow."

"It can snow up here any day in the year," Clay said. He brought in some wood for the fire. "Tim, why don't you dig up some of that muddy stuff by the lake, and we can put the fish between hunks of it and bake 'em. It's good that way."

"Mud?" Tim raised his eyebrows, but he went and got the stiff mud. There was a sharp wind ruffling the lake, and the day darkened. Huge clouds scudded across the sky.

"I'm sure sorry about holding us up, Clay," Perry said.

"Forget it," Clay said, "it could have happened to any of us. Anyway, in this weather it may be just as well to hole up for a bit." He sat back on his heels, surveying his fire. "I was thinking if it wasn't for the horses, we could use the boat and save a lot of time. If they were tame horses, we could guide them across—they could swim behind the boat—but I don't dare try it with the wild ones."

"What if somebody—whoever it was or whatever it was—lets the horses loose again?" Perry said.

"I don't think it will happen," Clay said. "But just to make sure, Tim and I can take turns watching them."

"I could watch, too, from the doorway," Perry said. "I can't move, but I could yell."

"O.K.," Clay said.

He touched the match to a heap of birch bark where the flame had gone out. It leaped up into orange flame and the sweet smoke filled the room for a moment. Clay went outside to clean the fish.

Later, when the fish were finally baked in their clay slabs, and Clay had picked the cranberries and made a sauce out of the berries and the last of the sugar, the boys ate hungrily.

"Can Bushman have a trout?" Perry asked.

"No, he might get some bones in his throat."

"I'll bone it for him," Perry said. Painstakingly he picked the bones out of his last fish.

"He makes out all right off the land," Clay said. "But you can give it to him if you want to. We've got more than plenty." He rubbed Bushman's velvety ear.

Perry held out the piece of fish to Bushman, and the whole thing disappeared in one gulp.

"Gosh," Perry said, "you'd think he'd at least show he enjoyed it. Chew it a little or something."

Clay laughed. "He enjoyed it."

"Those are darned good trout," Tim said. "I'll get some more tomorrow."

"I'm glad we have the boat," Clay said. "You know, I was thinking, if we rowed Perry across the lake, and then came back and took the horses around the lake, that would speed things up."

"Leave me alone over there?" Perry said. Then he added, "Well, that's O.K., if you have to."

"I could leave Tim with you," Clay said. "Then I could ride Chinook and lead the two horses, and save time, see? Otherwise, one of us has to walk all that way."

"I don't think that's such a hot idea," Tim said. "We should stick together."

"But it would save time."

"As long as you don't get lost, Clay," Perry said.

"All I have to do is follow the shore line till I get to you. Then we'll strike out from there for the river and for town. It shouldn't be too far to the river, at least."

"Joe must be worried about us," Perry said.

Clay nodded. "He'll probably send out help if we're gone much longer. The thing is, though, if they tracked us as far as where the avalanche was, they'd lose us there because they'd figure we couldn't have gone through into the meadow."

"Unless they sent an Indian," Perry said. "An Indian would notice that that was a recent avalanche, and he'd look in the meadow. That's how Indians are."

"You read too many books," Tim said.

The wind howled outside the cabin. "I'm going to watch the horses," Clay said. "You guys keep the fire going, O.K.? I'm running low on matches." He went outside and cut two stout branches from a pine and brought them in to Perry. He gave him his knife. "You could maybe make some crutches out of these, or canes, or something to lean on when you're able to get up."

"Sure," Perry said. "I'll try."

"I'll help him," Tim said.

Clay took his jacket and went down to the shore of the lake. He wanted to make sure that the boat was secure. Perry watched him from the cabin. Clay pulled the boat up on the shore and turned it over. He stood for a moment looking around. The wind whipped the pine branches. It was the closest to real darkness of any

75

night they had seen on this trip.

Clay untied the horses and brought them closer to the cabin. The stallion was restless, but the wild mare seemed played out. He talked to them, soothing them. The wind was making them nervous. Chinook shook her head, her mane flying. Clay had staked them out now in a place where there was at least a little grazing. Pea vine and false solomon's seal grew along the base of the trees.

Then as Clay took up his vigil near the horses, his back settled against a tree, Perry closed the cabin door and hopped back to his chair.

"Clay looks lonesome out there," he said.

"Well, we'd better keep watch," Tim said. "You never know."

On the lake a loon raised his lonely laughter. Perry shuddered. It was an almost human, insane sound.

Tim stared gloomily at the stove. "It's funny about all the stuff that's happened to us," he said. "It's almost enough to make a guy believe in ghosts."

"You sound like my mother," Perry said.

"Thanks a lot."

"There's no such thing as supernatural forces. What I'm scared of is this darned big wilderness. Who knows what's in it? There may be creatures men have never even seen. I mean this far from civilization and all . . ." His voice trailed off.

"Well, we've had some lucky breaks," Tim said. "The two cabins, the rope, the boat, the fishing gear, and all that." He thought for a minute. "Maybe some trapper is mad because we're on his land."

"But we were on Skookum Donahue's trap line," Perry said. "Mr. Fuller said so."

"Well, we might have gone off it. Maybe the Indians are mad at us for messing around out here. Some of the old-time trappers are still mad because the government regulated trap lines. They think the whole country is theirs."

"I suppose it is hard on the Indians," Perry said. "This was all theirs once."

Tim was silent for a few minutes. Then he said, "What do you really think it is that's after us?"

"I don't know," Perry said. "Maybe it's something like the Abominable Snowman."

"Do you believe in the Abominable Snowman?"

"Well, not really, I guess."

"Well, then . . ."

"Just because I don't believe in it doesn't say it couldn't exist. I'm a natural-born skeptic."

Tim thought about it. "I don't know if an Abominable Snowman could untie horses' ropes and stuff like that."

Perry shrugged. "Who knows what it could do."

"Clay says whatever it is has to be human."

"Clay doesn't know any more than we do," Perry said, but then he was sorry he had said it because it sounded disloyal to Clay. "Well, he believes in common sense," he added. "I guess he's right. But who would be after us?"

Tim yawned. "Well, none of us knows, so I guess we might as well stop trying to figure it out before we scare ourselves to death."

Perry let himself down onto the floor and made himself as comfortable as he could. Tim was already half asleep. Bushman lay stretched out at Tim's feet, snoring.

"Why do you suppose Bushman didn't hear whatever it was?" Perry asked.

"The wind made a lot of noise," Tim said sleepily. "Like tonight." The wind was slapping the loose boards of the cabin and a little way off the waves of the lake

lapped against the shore.

"Why didn't he smell it then?"

"Whoever it was was probably smart enough to stay downwind. Or maybe he knew the old Indian trick about standing in campfire smoke so there's no human smell."

They were quiet, and soon both of them slept.

Outside the stallion neighed and stepped sideways, cracking the brush under his feet. There was a smashing sound in the woods nearby. Clay yelled. Perry and Tim struggled to their feet. Tim got to the door first and threw it open. Perry hopped painfully behind him.

"What is it?" Tim yelled.

At that moment a huge bull moose emerged from the trees and headed for the lake. Bushman raced after him, barking furiously. The moose plunged into the lake and in a moment he was swimming steadily toward the middle of the lake, only his shoulders and his magnificent antlered head showing above the water.

"Oh, if I only had a gun!" Clay said.

Already the moose was only a dark speck on the lake. Perry looked up at the sky. Smoke from the cabin fire wreathed in the cool air. Clay turned up his collar and went back to his vigil and the two boys went back into the cabin.

When Clay came to get Tim to relieve him, he looked pale. "Wake up, you guys," he said. "I just went to see if the boat was O.K."

"What about it?" Perry said.

"It's got a hole stove in the bottom."

"Oh, no!" Tim said.

"Clay," Perry said. "How could it happen?"

"Maybe the moose stepped on it," Tim said.

"It looked as if it was hacked out with a hatchet," Clay said. He sat down on the birch chair and stared at the fire.

chapter 14

"WELL," CLAY SAID FINALLY, "I GUESS WE'RE NO WORSE
off than we were before we had a boat."

"No more fish," Tim said. "Unless we can cast from
shore and catch something."

"It's too marshy," Clay said.

"Never mind the boat," Perry said. "What I want to
know is, who's after us?" He was sitting on one of the
chairs, his leg straight out in front of him, resting on a
stump that Clay had found for him. His face was drawn
with pain and fear.

There was a pause. Then Tim said slowly, "I'd sure
like to know that, too."

"Whatever it is," Clay said, "it's *natural*. We've got to
get that through our heads."

"It makes no noise, it leaves no trace . . ." Perry said.

"And it carries a hatchet," Clay said.

Tim tried to laugh. "Yeah," he said, "how many ghosts
do you know that carry a hatchet?"

"There's no such thing," Clay said doggedly. "Anyway, what I've been thinking is, a moose has real sharp
hooves, like a horse. A cow moose could have done a

job like that, that would look like a hatchet had done it."

"Sure," Tim said. "It was probably a moose."

Clay said, "Because if the horses . . ." He jumped to his feet. "I forgot the horses!" He ran out of the cabin with Tim close behind him. The horses were grazing quietly.

"Clay," Tim said, "it's my turn to stand horse watch. Would you think it was O.K. . . ." He grinned sheepishly. ". . . if I sat right outside the cabin? I could get some heat from the fire, and I can see the horses from there."

"Tim," Clay said, "you don't go for that silly ghost idea, do you? I mean you got more sense . . ."

"Sure I have," Tim said. "I don't believe in ghosts. That's crazy. I just thought . . . it's a lot warmer near the fire and all."

"All right," Clay said, "but keep a sharp watch. We can't afford to lose the horses now, with Perry laid up."

"Don't worry, I'll watch like a hawk." Tim sounded relieved.

Clay went inside and threw himself down on the bed of branches. "I've got to get some sleep. Wake me up in about an hour, somebody, O. K.?"

"O.K.," Perry said.

"You ought to sleep, too, Perry."

"I couldn't sleep a wink," Perry said.

"Well, keep the fire going. I'm down to my last match."

"Sure," Perry said, only half listening.

The wind had driven the mosquitoes away and it was easy for Clay to fall instantly asleep. But he had hardly gone to sleep before Bushman's wailing woke him.

"Now what?" He came bolt upright.

"It's Bushman," Tim yelled. "He's brought home a porcupine."

"Oh, no," Clay moaned. He went outside. The woebegone Bushman stood beside the dead body of a porcupine, his head hanging.

"He's full of quills," Tim said.

"He never learns," Clay said. "Well, we'll have to get them out." He went back into the cabin and looked around. "I wish there were some pliers here."

"Can't we just pull them out?" Perry asked. "Poor old Bush."

"No. We can get a few that way, but they have barbs on them. If we don't get them all out, they could kill him."

Bushman was pawing at his face and whining.

Clay went outside and broke off a small green branch and turned it back upon itself. "Let's see if this will work." He looked at Bushman. "We'll have to rope his legs." He went into the cabin for rope, and securely tied the dog's legs. "Tim, you hold his head. He'll struggle so you'll really have to hold on."

"What can I do?" Perry said.

"Just stand by, for now. And watch the horses."

With Tim holding his collar tightly, Bushman let Clay yank some of the quills from his muzzle. Then the pain began to build up and the boys had to throw him to the ground. There were at least two hundred quills sticking out of his head. The ones that were hardest to get were those inside his mouth.

"Perry," Clay said, "if you can manage it, grab his jaws. Hold one jaw in each hand, with his lips over his teeth."

Perry tried, but it was hard for him to keep his balance. "If Tim can do that, I'll hold his collar."

Bushman let out a shuddering moan.

"Can't we let the last ones go?" Perry said. "Won't they work themselves out?"

"No," Clay said. "They have reverse barbs. They'd just keep working and holding deeper every time he moved his muscles."

At last he said, "This looks like the last one." Carefully he extracted it. "That's all."

Released, Bushman came unsteadily to his feet. He gave a feeble wag of his tail. Then he ran to the lake and plunged his muzzle into the water, his forelegs sinking in the marshy land. He bounded around the shore in sheer relief, and then he crowded up to the boys to be patted.

"Well, one good thing," Clay said, "we can have porcupine for breakfast."

"Aak!" Perry said.

"Sure. It's very good." Clay unsheathed his knife. He turned the porcupine over with his foot and deftly slit the exposed smooth belly. "See? Now it's easy to skin him. You just fold the skin back like a glove." As he skinned the animal, he said, "Or you can roast it unskinned and then the quills burn up. But you lose a lot of fat that way because it burns up, too. When you aren't sure where your next meal is coming from, it's important to get all the fat you can."

When the porcupine was done, even Perry had to admit that it was good.

"You know what I'd like right now?" Tim said, finishing off his portion of the meat. "One of my mother's salads."

Perry looked thoughtful. "I read this book," he said.

"Oh, you and your books!" Tim said. "Who can eat a book?"

But later in the day, when Clay had taken the horses out to the clearing to run them around the snubbing post, and when Tim was trying vainly to get close enough to the lake to cast out a fishing line, Perry hoisted himself out of his chair and, using the two canes he had made, he hopped outside. He kept glancing fearfully around, for he did not for a moment believe that it was a moose that had stepped through the boat. He had seen some things growing, however, and he wanted to take another look. He thought he recognized them.

Laboriously he moved down the slope toward the

lake. There was a sharp decline just before one reached the lake, and he stopped short of that. If he hadn't had a bad ankle, he would have scrambled down the decline without a second thought, but now he knew that if he went down, he would have trouble getting back. Anyway, what he was looking for grew on the top of the bank. He was quite sure it was something called fireweed, and he remembered from the book he had read that you could cut the stems and boil them in salted water. Some people called it wild asparagus.

His knife wasn't as good as Clay's, but it would do. Carefully lowering himself to the ground, he began to cut the young stalks. His ankle throbbed, but he tried not to notice it. He had faith in Clay's splint. He wished he could be like Clay. Clay could do anything.

When he had cut a big armful, he painfully got up again and gathered the weeds together, balancing himself precariously on his canes. Trying to clutch the fireweed under his arm and hold one of the canes in the same hand was troublesome, but after dropping the fireweed a couple of times he finally made it back to the cabin. Now he needed some water. Maybe Tim would get it for him. He could see him standing still by the water's edge. Tim was half turned toward shore and he seemed to be holding his arm back as if he were about to throw something. Perry felt alarm. Every unexpected thing was a source of terror. Tim's arm came way back and flung out, and then his voice rang out in a shout of triumph. He ran toward another spot on the shore, and then he came racing up to the cabin carrying a ptarmigan.

"I hit it with a rock!" he said. "Doggone, I winged it with a rock! Hey, we're really eating high off the hog today! Porcupine for breakfast and ptarmigan for lunch."

"If you'll get me some water," Perry said, proud that he could add his contribution, "we'll have greens, too."

"Those weeds?" Tim said. "You've got to be kidding." But he brought the water, and soon Perry had them cooking in the big iron pot he had unearthed in a corner of the cabin.

When Clay came back with the horses, the boys had a good meal ready. He ate heartily and then sat back on his heels and grinned at them. "Hey, you guys will make sourdoughs yet."

"You think you're the only one can cook?" Tim said. He winked at Perry.

"Those horses," Clay said, "are working out real good. They're not the brightest critters in the world, but they gentle easy." He took the pot down to the lake to clean it out.

"Those weeds were really good," Tim said to Perry.

Perry stretched out his aching leg and smiled. It was nice to know that he had done something right.

The wind continued to howl outside the little cabin, and in spite of the cozy fire, every noise made them uneasy. Tim sat just outside the open door keeping an eye on the horses, and Clay built up the fire. Perry tried to sleep, but it was impossible. He was too afraid of what might happen if he closed his eyes.

chapter 15

THE NIGHT PASSED WITHOUT INCIDENT, BUT WHEN CLAY turned in from his watch, he reported that it was snowing.

"Snowing in July!" Perry exclaimed.

"Anything can happen up here," Clay told him. He brushed big flakes off his jacket and put some more wood on the fire. "Be sure to keep the fire going."

"Are we low on matches?" Tim asked.

"All gone."

"Gosh," Tim said soberly, "that's bad."

"I guess I could start a fire without one if I had to," Clay said, "but it's kind of tricky and I'm not sure it would work."

He used the last of the flour and the dried apples for breakfast. "We're out of coffee," he said.

"We could make tea out of yarrow blossoms," Perry said. "There's yarrow growing in back of the cabin."

"Maybe there's something to be said for this book-reading after all," Tim said.

"I was hoping we could get going this morning," Clay said, "but we'll have to wait till the snow quits. Do you think you can ride, Perry?"

"Sure," Perry said. He was not as confident as he sounded, however. His ankle ached fiercely most of the time. But he was so anxious to get back to the settlement that it was worth any added pain.

"I sure wish we hadn't lost that boat," Clay said. He threw himself down on the bed and was instantly asleep.

Bushman was outside running wildly in the snow. He leaped and rolled and ran in wide circles, thoroughly enjoying himself.

"Perry, you watch the horses awhile," Tim said. "I want to explore." He was soon out of sight in the swirling snow.

The horses were dim shapes in the snow. Perry watched them so intently his eyes ached. Each time it was his watch, he was afraid something would happen to the horses and it would be his fault. He felt terrible about his ankle. If he hadn't been so clumsy, it wouldn't have happened.

He sat hunched forward in the doorway of the cabin, feeling the warmth of the fire at his back and the cold of the snow on his face. He blinked rapidly, keeping his eyes on the horses. From time to time he had to take off his glasses and wipe off the moisture. He wished Tim hadn't gone off. He felt terribly lonely. Clay was there, of course, but Clay was sound asleep. The horses looked so patient, with their heads down against the snow. Snow in July. The kids in Pasadena would never believe that. He took off his glasses again and wiped them and put them back on.

One of the horses whinnied, and Perry tensed. He got up, bracing himself against the side of the door. Suddenly the stallion moved, and Perry saw something. In the falling snow it was only a shadow, and it disappeared so quickly that he could hardly be sure he had seen it. He yelled and began to hop toward the horses, using his two canes. It was slippery and he almost fell.

Clay came bounding out of the cabin. "What is it?"

"I saw something over there behind the stallion."

"You stay here," Clay said. "You'll fall in this snow." He ran, sliding, toward the horses.

Perry watched him tensely. In a few minutes Clay came back. He shook his head. "There's nothing there now."

"I know I saw something."

"Probably you did."

"Aren't there any prints?"

"I couldn't find any. But the snow is falling so fast, and the area is all trampled up by the horses. Go on back in, Perry. I'll watch."

"You're supposed to be sleeping."

"Well, I'll watch awhile. I'm wide awake now. I can move faster than you can." He glanced around the cabin.

Just then they heard Tim yell and in a moment he burst into the cabin. "Hey, guess what! I just came across a fresh-killed bear cub. Looks like a moose killed it. There's tracks of a little moose and a cow, and then this bear. Anyway, I saw this big old owl swooping down and I moved in, and there it was. Hurry, Clay, help me cut it up and get some of it back here before the animals tote it all off."

"Are you sure it was a moose killed it?" Perry said.

"It's got to be, with those tracks. The thing is, we got all this terrific bear meat. Hurry up, Clay."

"O.K.," Clay said. "Perry, keep an eye on things for a little while. We'll hurry back."

"What about . . . what about what I saw out there?"

"What?" Tim asked.

"Perry thought he saw a shadow out around the horses."

"Did you find anything?" Tim asked.

"No."

"No tracks?"

"There's too much snow falling."

Tim clapped Perry on the back. "Don't worry. It was probably some animal, long gone. They won't hang around the horses. Anyway, it's easy to think you see things in the snow."

"But I did see it," Perry said.

"We won't be long, Perry," Clay said.

With a sinking heart Perry watched them go. But he made himself sit in the doorway, staring fixedly at the horses.

It seemed like a very long time that the boys were gone, and finally the snow stopped. Almost at once, as the sun came out, the ground snow began to melt. Snow dripped from the trees. Soon the earth was partly dark with moisture, partly patched with the last of the snow.

Perry was sleepy. He had to sit up very straight to keep himself from dozing. He wished the boys would come back. He hoped everything was all right. Maybe the dead bear was a trap. A trap set by whom? That was what upset him most, not knowing the identity of whatever plagued them.

He thought of the fire and turned back to look at it. It was burning low so he grasped his two canes and got up to replenish it. As he stood up, he glanced at the tiny window at the back of the cabin. His blood froze. There was a face in the window. A horrible grotesque face. It disappeared almost at once. With a scream of terror Perry hopped for the door. Using his canes he went across the slippery ground at a remarkable speed. His one thought was to get as far away from the cabin as he could. He leaped upon the snow-covered incline at the shore and felt himself falling. Instinctively he kept his injured leg up, but in spite of his desperate efforts to break the fall, he skidded down the incline to the very edge of the lake.

In the slide he lost one of his canes. After some struggling he managed, with the use of the remaining cane, to get up on his good foot. But to ascend the incline was impossible. Even with two useful feet it would have been a scramble. With one it was out of the question. He would have to stay where he was until the boys came back.

Sick with fear, and ashamed of himself for his panic, he let himself down onto the ground to wait. He tried to look in three directions at once. If whatever he had seen at the window came at him, he would fight it off with his cane. He shuddered uncontrollably. He had never seen such a face. It was . . . it was like an Egyptian mummy or something.

When the boys finally came, Perry was so glad to see them, he could have cried. He shouted until their faces appeared at the top of the incline.

"What the heck are you doing down there?" Tim said.

"I slipped," Perry said. "Clay, there was a face. At the window . . . there was a face peering in at me."

"Oh, come on." Tim sounded disgusted.

"Honest! It was a terrible face."

Clay looked at him coldly. "You let the fire go out," he said.

chapter 16

IN SILENCE THE TWO BOYS HELPED PERRY UP THE SLOPE
and back to the cabin. Perry looked in despair at the
gray ashes that had been a fire.

"I'm sorry," he said in a small voice.

"We've got all this bear meat to cook," Tim said ac-
cusingly.

"Maybe I can get a fire going," Clay said. He looked
around the cabin. "We'll have to wait till the sun is
bright. You guys might as well get some sleep. I'll watch
the horses for a while."

"Will Bushman get into the meat?" Tim asked.

"No. He doesn't like bear meat unless it's cooked."
Clay went outside.

"Tim," said Perry, "I really did see a face."

Tim looked at him doubtfully. "You might have
imagined it," he said.

"No, I saw it."

"There's a story about a face at the window," Tim
said. "They used to tell it at scout camp. About this
head of hair at the window. Only it turned out to be
a porcupine."

"This was no porcupine," Perry said. "This was a real face, only all painted and weird looking, like an Egyptian mummy or something."

"Oh, come on," Tim said. He curled up on half of the bed. "I'm going to sleep."

Perry sighed and eased himself onto the bed. He was sure they would never believe him. "But there is *something*," he whispered.

Tim rolled over and looked at him for a minute. "I guess there is," he said uneasily. "But it isn't any old painted mummy." He stared up at the ceiling. "I wish I knew what it was."

"Me, too," Perry said. In a way he felt better because Tim had admitted there was something—at least it wasn't just his imagination. But it was frightening, too, because Tim's believing it made it real. He lay staring into the half light, wishing he were back in Pasadena.

In spite of himself he dozed. He woke with a start when Clay came into the cabin. Clay shook Tim. "Tim, go watch for a while. The sun is up. I'll see if I can get a fire going." He held up a bottle. "I found a whiskey bottle out in back of the cabin. I'm going to see if I can start a fire with a piece of the glass."

Tim went out to the horses, and Perry hobbled to the doorway where he sat watching Clay. First Clay smashed the bottle on a rock. Then he heaped up on the ground the powdered structure of an old bird's nest and added wisps of birch bark. At one side he piled up some more birch bark, some conifer twigs, and a few pieces of heavier wood. The bird's nest and the birch bark were in bright sunlight. He held a piece of the glass directly over the pile, a few inches above it. He crouched there patiently, watching the heap intently. It didn't seem possible to Perry that anyone could start a fire this way. But suddenly there was a wisp of smoke.

"It's coming!" Perry said.

Clay didn't answer. He kept very still, not moving the glass at all. Then there was a tiny tongue of orange flame, and then another. There was a curl of black smoke. In a minute the birch bark was burning. Clay put down the glass and picked up one of the large pieces of bark in the bigger pile. It caught, and he replaced it. Soon the big pile was burning brightly.

"Watch it," he said to Perry. He ran inside with an armful of twigs and bark and piled them expertly in the stove. He came back and picked up a piece of burning wood and took it inside and lighted the fire in the stove. When it was burning steadily, he came back and stamped out the small fire outside. He looked at Perry and grinned. He had a streak of black soot across his cheek.

"We're in business!" he said.

Perry felt immensely relieved. It was the first time since he had let the fire go out that Clay had smiled at him.

"I'll cook the meat if you'll tell me how," he said.

"O.K.," Clay went around to the back of the cabin and began bringing the hunks of bear meat in.

"Do you cook it like steak?" Perry asked.

"No," Clay said. "It's too stringy. Besides, you should cook bear a long time to avoid trichinosis."

"Oh, I know what that is," Perry said. "You get it from underdone pork."

"Right. We'd better roast this meat. It'll take several hours. Do as much as you can do at a time."

"Should I trim off the fat?" Perry asked, looking at the meat the boys had skinned.

"No. There's only about half an inch. It's good for basting." Clay looked at Perry. "Will you be all right for a little while? I want to work out with the horses and Tim is going to help me."

Perry swallowed. "Sure," he said. In spite of himself he glanced at the window.

"It's daylight now," Clay said. "Nothing will bother you."

"O.K.," Perry said. But he watched uneasily as Clay went off down the path to the horses. In a few minutes even Bushman was gone. Perry busied himself with the meat. He found a big open pan that fitted in the oven, and he put as much of the bear meat into it, with the fat side up, as the pan would hold. There was quite a lot of meat left, and he was kept busy brushing off the blowflies that gathered.

"Stupid flies!" he muttered, waving his hat back and

forth over the meat. It occurred to him after a while that the flies flew low, close to the ground. If he could hoist the meat. . . . He looked up at the roof of the cabin. That might not be high enough. He hopped to the door and looked around outside. There was a lodgepole pine that he had noticed before, near the cabin. All its branches, up to a height of about twenty feet, had been trimmed off. Maybe for just this purpose. Anyway, it might work, if he could get the meat up there. He got a length of rope and tied up the meat. Then he took it outside and looked up at the tree. If he could flip the rope over the first branch . . . Clay could do it. Or Tim. Well, if they could do it, so could he—it just might take him a little longer.

He twirled the free end of the rope a few times and then tossed it at the branch. He missed by a wide margin. He tried again, his tongue clenched between his teeth. Six times he tried and missed. The seventh time the end of the rope looped around the branch. Then he had to hold up the meat and play out the rope until the free end of it dangled within reach. Triumphantly he got hold of it. Clay and Tim should see him now! He seized the rope and gave it a tug. He pulled so hard that he lost his balance and came down on his sprained ankle. The pain was so intense that it sent waves of nausea through him, and he let go of the rope, and dropped the meat. The end of the rope flew up out of reach.

When he felt the pain receding, he hauled down the

rope and tried again. Finally he made it, and this time he pulled more carefully. In a few minutes he had hauled the meat up almost as high as the twenty-foot branch.

"There!" he said aloud. "Success." He secured the rope to the trunk of the tree. Now the meat wouldn't get covered with flies. Clay would have to admit it was a pretty slick idea. They could leave it there till they were ready to cook it. Maybe he could even make a stew out of some of that meat. He began to look around for possible vegetables. He had read in that book that there were wild onions, but it was best not to pick them because sometimes a person could mistake them for something poisonous. But up in the back of the cabin he had seen what he thought was the yellow flower of the mustard plant. He decided to take a closer look.

First he checked the fire and added some fuel. The meat was beginning to cook. The fat was dripping into the pan. It smelled like a delicious roast beef. He gave it an experimental poke and decided it was doing well.

Depending on his canes for support he left the cabin and went to the place where he had seen the blossoms. Sure enough, they were, he was quite certain, black mustard. He recognized the flowers with their four petals and six little upright stamens, four long and two shorter. He tasted a leaf to make sure. Then he began picking the youngest plants, with their fuzzy leaves. What he'd do, he thought, was cut up some of the bear

100

meat, add water and some of the salt that was still left, cook it until it was tender, and then dump in some of the mustard to cook with it. He didn't know how it would come out, but it sounded like a good idea. If it was really good, maybe Clay wouldn't think he was such a stupid jerk. He'd melt some fat in the bottom of the kettle first, and brown the meat before he added the water. He hung around the kitchen a lot at home, and that was the way their housekeeper made a stew when his mother wasn't there. When his mother was home, she did the cooking, but she was gone a lot. He took off the sweater that his mother had knitted for him, and filled it with the young mustard plants, and started back to the cabin.

On the way back it occurred to him that their enemy, whoever it was, might have gone into the cabin and put the fire out! Panic-stricken, he half limped, half slid across the pine needles to the cabin. But everything was all right. The fire was burning properly, and the meat smelled wonderful. Relieved, he sank down on a chair and began breaking up the mustard plants into smaller pieces. When he finished that job, he went out to gather more plants that he had seen.

Finally Tim and Clay came back, Clay riding the little mare. "Look at her," he called to Perry. "She's more than half broke already. Now two of us can ride." He slid off her back and tied her to a tree, patting her and murmuring to her.

"That's great," Perry said. "How about the stallion?"

"I haven't got very far with him yet."

"We ought to name them," Perry said.

"O.K. You name them. You're the literary man."

Perry thought for a minute. "How about Storm for the stallion and Cloud for the mare?"

"Good enough." He patted the mare's nose. "You like your name, Cloud?"

She whinnied and caught his sleeve in her teeth.

"My gosh," Tim said, "that bear meat is the best-smelling stuff I ever smelled. I'm starved."

Perry removed the meat from the fire. It bubbled and sizzled deliciously.

"Let's eat," Tim said.

"What's this?" Clay pointed to some greens.

"Scurvy grass," Perry said. "Make believe it's a salad."

Tim took a mouthful. "It would be better with dressing."

Clay tried the bear meat. "Hey, this is great."

Perry beamed.

Clay went to the door and whistled. "I haven't seen Bushman for a couple of hours." But before he had finished saying it, Bushman came loping out of the woods. "He smelled the meat, too," Clay said. He broke off a piece and tossed it to Bushman. The dog swallowed it in one gulp and pawed Clay's knee begging for more. "I guess there's enough." Clay gave Bushman another big piece. "Did you cook it all, Perry?"

Proudly Perry pointed to the cache up in the tree. "I didn't have room for all of it, and the flies were getting at it."

Clay looked at the tree and then he looked at Perry. "You're getting to be a regular woodsman," he said. "Look at that, Tim."

"Great," Tim said, with his mouth full. "Let's give Perry a medal for good cooking when we get back."

"Which reminds me," Clay said. "I think we're about ready to move."

"Now?" Perry was dismayed. "I want to make a stew out of the meat that's left. I got some black mustard to go with it; it'll be real tasty."

"Let's wait till tomorrow," Tim said. "That'll give me time to make the travois, and Perry can make his stew. We can take the rest of the cooked meat with us."

"All right," Clay said. "Tim is going to make a travois for you to travel in."

"What's a travois?" Perry asked. He looked doubtful when Tim explained it to him. "It'll be better than riding," Tim said.

For the rest of the afternoon Tim worked on the travois, cutting long poles to serve as runners, and shorter pieces for cross-pieces. He thatched the seat to make it as comfortable as possible.

While Tim worked on the travois and Clay went off in the woods to chart a course, Perry got the meat down from the tree and went to work making a stew. He felt useful now, and he was happier than he had been on the whole trip.

At suppertime all three boys were as hungry as if they had not already eaten large quantities of roast bear. The stew was very good, and they ate all of it except a bowlful that went to Bushman.

They went to bed early, to get a good night's sleep before starting on their way. A little before midnight Clay woke Perry to take over the watch. Perry went outside and sat down near the horses, his back to a tree. The night had cooled off, and he shivered. It made him very nervous to be out there alone, even though Tim and Clay were within earshot. He wished the light would come. It seemed darker than usual. He leaned back and closed his eyes. Then he jerked his head up; he had been dozing. He looked guiltily at the horses, but they were standing quietly. Silently he scolded himself. What if something had happened to them just when they were about to leave for home, and all because he fell asleep? He sat up straighter, feeling the hard bark of the tree pressing against his back. It hurt a little, but that would keep him awake.

He looked up at the sky. It looked as if dawn was coming, and he was glad of that. Then he looked again. The light that he saw was in the north. That was the wrong place for the sun to be rising. And the light was strange, as if a searchlight was playing on the sky. As he watched in alarm, the whole northern sky lighted up in great shafts of brilliance. Masses of light widened and deepened.

"Clay!" Perry shouted. "Clay! Come here!" He was too frightened to move. The horses tugged restlessly at their ropes and whinnied. "Clay!" Perry called again. The lights were terrifying. Then suddenly it came to him, and he sank back against the tree sheepishly.

Clay and Tim came sleepily to the cabin door.

"What's the matter?" Clay asked.

"I thought you'd want to see the northern lights," Perry said.

The two boys came out and looked up at the sky.

"Hey," Tim said. "I've never seen them that good."

Together the boys watched until at last the lights began to fade from the sky. Soon after they were gone, the true dawn came. Tim and Clay went back into the cabin for more sleep, and Perry sat out his watch, too excited now by what he had seen to fall asleep.

chapter 17

THE NEXT MORNING THEY ATE SOME COLD ROASTED BEAR meat for breakfast, and drank some of Perry's spruce tea. Then Tim hitched the travois to Chinook. Clay wrapped the remaining cooked meat in ferns and put it in his pack. Reluctantly he put out the fire.

Perry hobbled over to the travois and looked at it.

"You face backward in it," Tim told him. "In fact, you'd better lie down. It will be more comfortable."

Perry lowered himself onto the travois. He didn't like the idea of not being able to see where he was going, but he had to admit that it would be more comfortable than trying to ride Chinook. When he let his leg hang down straight, his ankle throbbed fiercely.

Tim mounted Chinook, and after a few minutes Clay persuaded Cloud to let him mount her. He was leading Storm on a rope. Storm objected at first, but then he quieted down.

With Clay in the lead they started out, following the lake shore. Goodbye, cabin, Perry thought, watching it disappear. He hated to see it go—it had sheltered them well.

The travois was far from comfortable. Perry felt every bump up and down his spine. He tried to think of other things to take his mind off it, but it wasn't easy. He thought about Pasadena and about what his friends would be doing now. Going to the beach, probably. Surfing. If he were there, he might go to the beach with them, but he would be more likely to stay on the sand and read a book than to surf. Surfing scared him. I've got to get over being so scared of things, he told himself sternly. Clay and Tim don't panic. He seized the sides of the travois and tried to lift himself a little, to avoid the worst of the bumps. But his wrists soon grew tired. He hoped Clay knew where he was going.

Clay took out his compass often and checked his course. The shore of the lake jogged and jutted in all directions. It was impossible to see the mountains. Once they got on the other side of the lake, it should be easier. If they could just get to the Spirit River, there would be no more problems.

They were moving well. Clay seemed pleased with Cloud. She shied when a branch flicked across her face or when a squirrel skittered out of her way, or especially when Bushman raced close to her heels, but on the whole she was as steady as if she had been trained when she was a colt. She was a pretty little thing. Clay occasionally reached down and patted her rich brown coat.

"She's doing fine," he said once. "I wish we could have brought back all of Joe's horses."

In the middle of the morning Clay stopped for a moment to consult his compass. As far as he could tell, they were all right. They all hoped that in a few more hours they would reach the Spirit. After that they would have plain sailing.

Tim helped Perry get up so he could stretch for a few minutes. It was a pleasant place to stop. There was a mossy spot under the trees and the sunlight fell on it in a dappled pattern. The air was pungent with pine in the hot sunshine.

Bushman made use of the pause to dash off in pursuit

of a red squirrel. It amused Perry that the dog was always careful not to actually catch a squirrel. It was a pleasant game.

"I wish we had some drinking water," Perry said.

Clay was thirsty, too. "We'll probably come to water pretty soon." It was surprisingly hot after the coolness of the night, and the mosquitoes were bad. The horses' sides were dark with sweat. Perry hoped the bear meat wouldn't spoil. He was glad he had had time to cook it all.

After they had rested for a few minutes, they went

on again. Clay walked now, leading Cloud. Tim still rode Chinook.

"I hear water," Tim said after a while.

They stopped and listened and they all heard a sound like a waterfall. They hurried on, and in a few minutes they came out on a cliff. Just below them the water plunged in a foamy torrent over a falls into a churning white pool of water. The river was only about a dozen feet wide, but too rough to cross.

"What a pretty waterfall," Perry said. He got to his feet stiffly and walked to the edge of the cliff. The sunlit water sparkled and danced as it poured over the falls.

"Maybe it's the Spirit River," Tim said. "In which case, we're almost home."

"No," Clay said. He stood frowning uncertainly. "It can't be the Spirit so soon, and besides it's not wide enough."

"Well, it's good for a drink anyway," Perry said. "Look, there's a slopy place over there where we can get down to the water."

They walked over to the place he was pointing to.

"I'll help you down," Tim said to Perry. "Come on, Clay."

"In a minute," Clay said. "I want to take a look at the compass." He tied the horses and took out the compass and laid it on a tree stump. He studied it carefully as the other two boys went down to the river.

"Come on, Clay," Tim's voice sounded faint in the thunder of the falls. He and Perry splashed enthusiastically in the cold water.

Clay went to the place where the boys were and came down to join them. They were washing their hands and faces in a little pool made by some rocks. Tim stuck his whole head in. "I'd like a swim," he said, "but it's too darned cold and too swift. Boy, is it good to drink though!"

Perry lay down on his stomach and drank from the cold water. Its coldness made his head throb for a moment. When he had had enough, he splashed it over his head and face again. It felt good.

"This is a nifty place," he said. "Let's stay awhile."

Clay sat down on the hard sand and stared at the water. "We've got a problem," he said.

"What now?"

"To be going in the right direction we ought to cross this river. But we can't here. It's too swift. And the cliff is too steep for you, and maybe even for the horses. Unless we can find a crossing upstream, we'll have to go far out of our way."

Perry's face fell. "I thought it was such a great discovery. Good drinking water and all. How far do you think we'll have to go out of our way, Clay? I'm sore all over from that travois."

"Do you want to try riding?"

"All right," Perry said. "It couldn't be any more uncomfortable." To Tim he said, "It's a nice travois, Tim. It's just that the ground is so bumpy."

"Maybe we'll come to a place where we can ford the river just a little ways up," Tim said.

"Maybe," Clay said. "We'd better get going."

Perry groaned, but he got to his feet with Tim's help. The two boys boosted him up the bank and they all walked back to the horses. Bushman was sprawled out panting in the sun, just back from another squirrel chase, but he leaped up expectantly when they came up.

"I'll water the horses," Clay said.

"I'll give you a hand," Tim said.

They led the horses down the slope to the river where they drank noisily. Bushman joined them, but except for a couple of noisy slurps, he stayed back from the water. It was too cold.

When they came back again, Clay shouldered his pack and helped Perry onto Chinook's back. Perry winced as he felt the downward strain on his ankle and wondered as Tim untied the travois, if he had made a mistake. Tim was obviously disappointed that his idea had turned out badly.

When they were finally ready to start out, Clay went over to the stump where he had left his compass, but he didn't return. Instead, he just stared at the stump. Then he felt around the base of it.

"What's the matter?" Tim asked.

"My compass. I left it on this stump. It's gone."

"Gone!" Perry said. "The compass? Oh, no!"

Clay went through his pockets. "I know I left it here." He got down on his knees and searched more thoroughly on the ground.

"It might have been another stump," Tim said.

"There isn't any other stump."

Clay checked his pockets again. Then he looked in his pack.

"Bushman might have knocked it off," Perry said.

"Then where is it?"

"Maybe it fell over the cliff."

Clay stared down at the torrent of water. "If it did, it's gone for good."

The boys looked at each other.

"Boy," Tim said disgustedly. "How could you lose a compass?"

"I don't know," Clay said. He sounded angry and upset.

"There's always the sun," Perry said. He didn't want Tim and Clay to be angry.

Clay looked up. The sun had passed the zenith and already it was moving out of sight behind the tall trees.

chapter 18

THEY MOVED ALONG THE RIVER IN SINGLE FILE, CLAY
leading the way on Cloud, Perry following on Chinook,
and Tim at the end of the line leading Storm. Even Bushman was tired. Mosquitoes bothered them, and the flies
buzzed around the horses' ears. They walked for a long
time, and the river showed no sign of calming down so
they could ford it. It had widened out some, but it was
still a fast-moving torrent, too swift even for the horses.

Perry knew Clay was worried. The river was taking
them out of their way. It was the first time on the trip
that Clay had seemed really frightened. He looked back
over his shoulder at Perry. Perry looked at Clay anxiously, hoping he was going to stop.

"Pretty soon now, Perry," Clay said. "Not much
longer. I just want to get as far as we can make it before
we quit for the night."

"Sure," Perry said. But he winced and gasped with
pain as Chinook stumbled over a root.

In a few minutes Clay held up his hand. "Let's camp
here."

"Whew!" Tim said. "It's about time." He tied the stallion and went to help Perry off Chinook. "How you doin', pardner?"

"All right," Perry said in a muffled voice. He slid to the ground and stood balanced with the toe of his lame foot on the ground. "It's good to get off." He put a hand on Tim's shoulder to brace himself.

Clay had picked a place where the land sloped down to the river in a gentle grassy patch. There was a sandy beach.

When they had unloaded and the horses had been watered and tied, the boys lay down on the grass to rest.

"I don't know which I'm more of," Tim said, "tired or hungry."

"The meat is in my pack," Clay said. "We'll have to eat it cold." He pushed the pack toward Tim, and Tim opened it. He spread some of the meat out on top of the pack, and the boys helped themselves. Hungry though they were, they were almost too tired to eat.

"Eat even if you don't feel like it," Clay said. "We have to keep up our strength."

When they had eaten and had drunk some of the icy water, they felt better. Even Clay's worry receded a little. They lay back and talked.

"What would you have to eat if you had your choice of everything in the world?" Tim asked.

Perry thought it over carefully. "A hot fudge sundae from Wil Wright's."

"Who's Wil Wright?"

"A chain of ice cream places in California. They make the best ice cream in the world. What would you have, Tim?"

"Turkey," Tim said, "white meat, with gravy and cranberry sauce and salad. How about you, Clay?"

Clay laughed. "You're just torturing yourselves."

"But what would you have?"

"The biggest Hershey bar in the world," Clay said. "With almonds."

They were silent, thinking of food and home.

"How long do you reckon it will take us to get back?" Perry said at last.

"I don't know," Clay said. "I'll get us out as fast as I can, Perry."

"I know that. It's sure lucky we have you. Isn't it, Tim?"

"Yeah," Tim said, "but I guess we'd make it sooner or later."

"Not without Clay," Perry said. "I wouldn't, anyway."

"Let's get some sleep," Clay said. He whistled to Bushman, who was nosing gingerly along the water's edge. "Come on, boy. Keep me warm." Bushman bounded up to him and lay down, pushing with his nose.

In spite of their fatigue the boys got little sleep. The mosquitoes came down in swarms and made them miserable. Clay showed Perry how to bury his legs under mounds of grass and pine needles, but the insects still flew and buzzed around the boys' heads and arms. Soon all three of them were covered with itching bites. The horses, too, were restless.

When it was his turn to watch, Clay walked up and down the beach, stopping often to douse his head and arms in cold river water. Wakeful, Perry sat and watched him. He studied the North Star, checking their position. As far as he could tell, they would be all right, once they crossed the river. Toward morning, the wind changed from the prevalent West into the East. The birds and insects began flying low. Clouds appeared in the sky.

If they were in for cloudy weather, there would be no sun and no North Star to guide them, nor would Clay be able to start a fire with the piece of broken glass he kept in his pocket.

They ate hastily of the cold bear meat and started on their way. The clouds continued to pile up, and after a while Clay had to admit that he had no way of knowing whether they were on the same course or not. There was nothing to do but to follow the winding river and hope for the best.

chapter 19

LATE IN THE DAY THE RIVER BEGAN TO NARROW. THE current was still swift, but the water did not look quite as deep and as turbulent as it had been. Clay stopped and studied it.

"We've got to get across this river sooner or later," he said. "We're going away from our direction all the time we follow it. I'm going to see if I can ride Chinook across." He helped Perry down from the horse. He stroked her broad, glossy shoulder for a moment and then he mounted her. "You fellows wait here and we'll see what happens."

"Be careful," Perry said.

Clay guided the horse into the stream. The water churned and foamed around her slender legs. The river grew deeper toward the middle and soon it was up to her withers. Clay could feel the pull of the current as Chinook braced herself against it.

"Good girl," Perry said to her. "Keep going now. We'll make it."

The horse soon was chest-high in the water, but she kept going steadily. In a few minutes the water began to drop, and then they were on the other side. Clay waved triumphantly to Tim and Perry. Then he rode Chinook back again. He leaned forward and put his face against her neck. "Good old dependable horse."

He slid off her back. "Tim, you and Perry ride across on Chinook. I'll bring the other two."

Chinook made the return trip with no trouble. With Cloud it was not so easy. She was skittish of the water and tried to pull back. Talking to her all the way in a low, soothing voice, Clay finally got her across. Then he led Storm, who followed with no resistance. The white hairs in Storm's reddish coat were dusty from the long trip, and he seemed to enjoy the cold splash of the water.

It took quite a while to coax Bushman across, but when Clay threatened to go off and leave him, he finally plunged, shuddering, into the cold stream, and swam to the other side. He floundered out and shook himself violently, spraying them all. Then he looked at Clay with reproach. Clay laughed and rubbed Bushman's shaggy wet head. "Sorry, boy," he said.

"Well, we're across the river," Perry said.

Clay looked happy. "Right. It's a relief. Now we can head for the Spirit River."

"Which way?" Perry asked.

Clay hesitated. He looked up at the sky. It was still a mass of swirling gray clouds. It looked as if it might rain. He had nothing to depend on now but his sense of direction. "This way," he said firmly, striking off at an angle, away from the river and somewhat back.

They rode for about an hour before he decided that it was time to stop for the night. They were deep in the woods now, and he picked a relatively clear place.

"We're down to the last of the bear meat," Tim said. "There's enough for tonight and that's all."

"I'll look for some greens," Perry said. He hobbled off.

"I'll look around, too," Tim said. He went off in the opposite direction.

When Perry came back with what he had found, Clay was looking for equipment to start a fire. He was going to have to use the Boy Scout method. He got out his hatchet and found first a well-seasoned stick of poplar about half an inch in diameter and about a foot long. That would serve as a drill. Then for a fireboard he split out part of a dry poplar branch. He cut a socket to hold the drill against a hollow in the fireboard. Then he cut a bow. He needed a thong now to loop around the drill. He looked around. Then it occurred to him to use his boot lace. He piled up a heap of twigs and bark for the fire. Then by moving the bow back and forth and rotating the drill in the fireboard he finally got enough friction to cause a spark. He blew on it hard, and it caught. He sat back on his heels and watched it. The smoke smelled good. "Now if we just had something to cook . . ." he said. But at least they had the fire for warmth. He packed away the equipment for further use.

"We can cook my greens."

"What have you got?"

"Nettles."

"Nettles! Now don't tell me nettles are good to eat."

"Sure. They're supposed to be very good." Perry looked at his wrists. "I got scratched up some."

"Nettles are prickly. How can we eat them?"

"Young nettle leaves and even the whole plants are good when you cook them," Perry said. "They lose their prickliness, like artichokes."

Clay shook his head in amazement. "It's a good thing you read. The last thing I'd think of eating would be nettles."

Perry rummaged around in his pack until he found the frying pan. "There's a spring over there," he said. "I'll get some water."

By the time he had returned, they heard Tim coming. He was whistling.

"He sounds successful," Clay said.

Tim lifted his arm. He was carrying a pair of partridge. He broke into a run. "It's our lucky day. They just sat there and let me hit them with a rock. And you've got a fire!"

"And delicious greens," Clay said, winking at Perry.

They cooked the birds and the nettles and ate them

hungrily, saving the bear meat for another time.

That night, with the wind to keep the mosquitoes off, they slept. And in the morning they started off in high spirits. Perhaps today they would come to the Spirit River.

chapter 20

By the middle of the day Clay admitted that he was lost. The forest rose around him in a solid wall and he did not know which way to turn. At one point they all realized with a shock that they had gone in a full circle.

By the time night came, Perry was really worried. "We should have come to the Spirit by now, shouldn't we?" he said to Clay, anxiously.

Clay nodded.

"How lost are we?"

"Just temporarily," Clay said. "We'll get out of this tomorrow."

After they camped, Clay said, "I want to scout around a bit. Will you watch the horses, Tim?"

"Perry can watch them," Tim said. "I want to look for food."

It made Perry nervous to be left alone, but he didn't say so. By now he was able to bear a little of his weight on his injured ankle so he busied himself straightening up the camp. He was sore from sleeping on the ground the last couple of nights and he decided to try to make a bed like the ones Clay had made. He borrowed Clay's knife.

When the boys had gone, he started cutting branches for the bed. It was not as easy as it looked. He worked hard, hacking away at branches and trying to weave them into a bed as he had seen Clay do. They kept springing free and hitting him in the face. Irritated, he tried to hold down some while he bent others into place.

Suddenly a blood-chilling yell split the air. He leaped up. At first he thought it was Tim making a joke. But it was repeated, close at hand, and Tim would be much farther away than that by now. Without thinking, Perry dived into the woods and ran, limping heavily again on his sore ankle. He came to a small clearing and stopped. His breathing was so loud that it came to him like a sound from another person. Still, frightened as he was, he knew he had to go back. Clay had left the horses in his charge. They couldn't lose those horses now. Whatever was trying to get them had to be driven off. Trembling he forced himself to run, yelling, through the woods.

"Go away!" he shouted. "Here I come. Go away!" He wished desperately that he had a gun, or even Clay's hatchet. All he had was the scout knife. He held it open in his palm like a dagger.

Breathless and limping, he came back to the camp site. The horses were still there, but Chinook's rope had been cut loose. Perry grabbed it, looking all around him. "Get out of here, whoever you are!" he yelled. "Get away from here!" There were soft footprints in the ground.

He stood still, panting and frightened, though there was no one to be seen. In a few minutes Clay returned. He looked at Perry in amazement. "What in the world are you doing?"

Perry told Clay what had happened.

Clay looked serious. He examined the prints. "From now on, we'll stay in two's to watch the horses." He gave Perry a quick pat on the shoulder. "It was brave to come back and protect the horses."

"I almost didn't," Perry said. "I was almost too scared."

"It's doing something when you're really scared that's brave," Clay said. And Perry remembered that his father had said that. He felt better.

As soon as Tim got back, Clay started them on their way again. It was late, and they were all tired and hungry. Tim had not found anything to eat. But Clay felt they should not stay where they were and the nights were almost as light as the days. They had a snack of bear meat, enough to keep them going. And they tried to keep from thinking about food.

After a long time Clay let out a shout. He turned to call back to the other two. "There's something up ahead. Looks like a cabin." Perry was riding Chinook and Tim was leading the stallion. They made themselves hurry, as Clay went ahead of them into a little clearing.

Perry leaned forward so he could see Clay, and as he did, his head brushed something in the tree above him. He looked up and shrieked. Just above his head, resting upon the branches, was a skeleton.

Tim yelled, too, and Clay hurried back to see what was the matter.

Perry slid off Chinook's back. "It's a skeleton," he whispered.

"It is, Clay." Tim's face was pale and his freckles stood out.

Clay rode up under the tree and looked at the skeleton. "A skeleton can't hurt you," he said. "Anyway, it's an animal, not a person."

"But how did it get in a tree?" Perry was backed away from it, leaning against Chinook's reassuring bulk.

Clay rode all around it, studying it. "It's a steer," he said. "What would a steer be doing out here?"

"How did it get into a tree?" Perry said again.

"I know," Clay said suddenly. "It must have got caught in a blizzard. The snow could easily drift in here to that height. It died in the blizzard, and when the snow melted, the skeleton stayed wedged in the branches."

"Snow that deep?" Perry said.

"Easy," Clay said. "Even in Montana we get it that deep. Come on, let's see what's up ahead." He turned Cloud's head and led the way into the clearing.

As the boys left the woods and came into the clearing, they saw a strange sight. Strewn all over the meadow in front of them were bones, bleached white. It looked like a graveyard.

"I don't like it," Perry said. "Let's get out of here."

Clay picked up a big white bone. "This must have been a cattle ranch. A herd of cattle died here, probably over the winter."

"Who would have a cattle ranch out here?" Tim asked.

"Maybe we're nearer to town than we thought," Clay said. "Come on, let's take a look around." He looked so cheered up that even Perry reluctantly followed him.

They picked their way over countless skeletons and heaps of bones toward what Clay thought was a cabin. When they came close to it, they found it was the caved-in remains of a ranch house. The roof had given way in the middle and the two ends of the house were all that still stood. The boys dismounted and poked around in the ruins.

"There's enough shelter to camp out in," Clay said. "We can spend the rest of the night here." He disappeared. "Hey," he called back, "there are cooking utensils."

"All we need is something to cook," Tim said.

They prowled around the ruins for a long time, turning up pots and pans and the remains of a fireplace. Clay even found a tin box half full of matches.

"There's a brook back there," Tim said. "I'm going to catch us some fish." He took out the fish hook and line he had brought from the last cabin and went down the overgrown path to the brook.

Perry helped Clay prepare beds inside the shelter of the canted roof. After a while Tim came back with a good catch of grayling. He cleaned them while Clay built the fire. They ate hungrily, but there were more fish than even they could eat. Clay cooked them anyway and packed them in fern leaves inside his pack for breakfast. "Cold fish will taste good," he said.

But while they tried to sleep, Bushman was restless. He got up often and prowled around the place, growling deep in his throat. The boys kept a close watch on the horses. Once Clay thought he heard something or someone in the bushes back of the ranch house, but when he looked, he could find nothing.

chapter 21

NEXT MORNING CLAY LEFT PERRY AND TIM WITH THE horses, and he went out on foot to scout the territory. He wanted to see where Tim's brook went.

He came back about an hour later with good news, the brook ran into a river, and he was pretty sure the river must be a tributary of the Spirit.

They hated to leave their shelter, but they packed up and set out again. They had some cold fish for breakfast, and there was still a little bear meat left.

"We'll eat the rest of the bear meat today," Clay said. "It won't keep much longer."

"Then what?" Perry asked.

Clay shrugged. "Something will turn up. It has so far. Maybe we'll be close to home."

The cloudy skies had cleared and Clay was able to get some sense of direction from the sun. They had wandered so far off course, he was not exactly sure which way they ought to go, but the brook seemed to take them in what ought to be the right way.

They followed the brook as it rushed over rocks. The woods grew thicker again and sometimes they waded in the brook to avoid the dense trees. In a little less than an hour they came to the river.

"If this really runs into the Spirit," Clay said, "we're set."

Perry did not completely understand why Clay thought it would run into the Spirit, but he accepted the idea that it might. His ankle was aching badly, and he was hungry. He had learned, however, that complaining only made things seem worse. He studied the river as they moved along its banks, trying to keep his mind on how pretty it was. It was a swift-moving stream about eight feet wide. The water was very clear and the gravel at the bottom was golden brown in the sun. Bushman stopped to take frequent drinks, careful not to let any water get above his muzzle. If only they weren't lost and hungry, Perry thought, it would be a lovely day.

"We'll have fish for supper," Tim said. "I hope you guys aren't sick of fish."

"Which reminds me," Clay said, "let's break for lunch."

The bear meat was somewhat the worse for time and travel, but it was not actually spoiled. They ate it, glad they had it. Afterward they took time for a quick bath in the cold river. They felt better after that.

"We'd better get going," Clay said.

They traveled farther that day than any day so far. Perry was so tired by late afternoon he didn't think he could sit on Chinook another minute. Every muscle ached. Finally, when it seemed he could not last any longer, Clay said, "Let's camp here." Perry slid off Chinook and collapsed in a little heap on the ground.

"Not a minute too soon," he said.

Clay took care of the horses, and Tim took off his boots and waded in the stream. "I'm going to fish awhile," he told Clay. He waded out and gathered up his gear.

Clay shrugged irritably. Then he caught himself and said, "Sure, Perry and I will make camp." And then, as Perry groaned and got to his feet, Clay added, "No, that's all right. Rest if you want to. There's no hurry."

So while Perry rested, Clay gathered wood for the fire. "We can sleep up on the stream bank," he said.

Clay stopped and wiped the perspiration from his face. The sun was still hot.

"Do you think we're going to run into the Spirit?" Perry asked him.

"I hope so. We seem to be going in the right direction. I hope the sun stays out."

"May the sun stay out and the enemy stay away," Perry said. He lifted a handful of pine needles and let them trickle through his fingers. They felt nice and prickly. The sun streamed down through the branches of the pine and across his face. It felt good to lie still. There was a smell of crushed mint, and near him a procession of tiny toads hopped along the bank.

"We'll keep double watch on the horses," Clay said.

"You know, whatever it is could have hurt us long ago if it meant to. It hasn't."

"Why do you say 'it'?" Perry asked.

"I said 'it' because I don't know who it is. I just can't figure it."

"Does it scare you?"

"Sure it scares me."

Clay found some birch bark and peeled it off to add to the heap of kindling.

"There are some dandelions over there," Perry said. "Want some for supper?"

"Sure." Clay threw himself on the ground. "If I catch a little sleep, will you watch the horses?"

"All right." Perry moved over to the patch where the dandelions were and started digging them out with the knife. The horses were close by, chewing contentedly on the leaves and bushes.

The ground was hard and Perry had to work to get the dandelions up, but at last he had a big heap of them. After washing them off in the stream and cleaning out the stringy-looking pieces, he got the pot they had brought from the ranch house and filled it with water. Now he had done his part. He sat down to wait for Tim. He hoped Tim would have luck fishing.

Clay still lay stretched out on the ground, sound asleep, so Perry decided to take a bath in the river. He stripped and stepped in. The water was icy and it rushed against his legs, almost knocking him over. Minnows

swimming in the shallows bumped against his legs. But
he kept on, stepping gingerly because the bottom was
gravel. He walked out to the middle of the stream,
crouched down and gasped as he felt the cold water
wash against his stomach and chest. He wished he had a
cake of soap. He thought longingly of the hot shower at
home, but all he could do was splash himself all over
until his skin glowed pink. Then he came out. He felt
fine.

Clay turned over and opened his eyes. "Hey, that
looks like a good idea," he said sleepily. He sat up and
began pulling off his boots. "Is it cold?"

"Yes," Perry said, "but it feels great."

Clay folded his clothes neatly and ran into the river. He yelled as the cold water splashed over him. Perry sat on the bank and watched him. It was a splendid time. In spite of all the difficult things that had happened to them, Perry knew he would remember moments like this.

Before Clay came out of the river, Tim came noisily downstream, splashing in the shallows, triumphantly waving a string of rainbow trout, big ones. "We eat again!"

Clay got dressed at once and lighted the fire. Perry put the pot of dandelions on to cook, and Tim cleaned the fish that they would want for supper. There were some left over, so he made a dammed place at the edge of the stream and put the extra fish there to keep till morning. Then after he got some green willow sticks and speared the fish, each boy took one and held it over the fire, turning it slowly. Soon they had a delicious meal.

They all felt exceptionally good after it was over. Clay piled more wood on the fire and they sat around it and sang all the songs they could think of. Clay sang off key, and Tim's voice broke occasionally, but Perry sang in the school glee club and he made up for the others. When they had tired of singing, he sang "The Streets of Laredo" and "On Springfield Mountain". As the fire finally died down, they were all pleasantly sleepy.

"I'll take the first watch," Tim said.

"I think two of us ought to watch," Clay said.

"Why? We're all right here. Whoever watches only has to yell out."

"All right," Clay said. He and Perry settled themselves as comfortably as possible and quickly went to sleep.

Perry was awakened by Clay shortly after midnight. The night was shadowy, like twilight perhaps, although he wasn't sure because in California they had no real twilight. He wished his watch had come when the light was brighter. He moved closer to the horses. Chinook whinnied a greeting. Perry had grown fond of Chinook on the trip. He got up and went over to rub her nose. "If I had a lump of sugar, I'd give it to you," he told her. She snorted and caught his hand with her lower lip. "Aak, you slobberer," he said. He patted her.

At that moment he heard a sound. He shouted and plunged toward it. He was not going to run away this time. In a moment he could hear Clay and Tim behind him. He pushed aside the branches of a pine, one snapped back and lashed him across the face, stinging his eye. At the same instant he saw there beyond the tree, alert and beautiful, a young buck. His antlers were held high. He stared at Perry with startled eyes, then in a silent bound he was gone.

Tim and Clay came panting up behind him, and Bushman raced off after the buck.

"What is it?" Clay said. He looked worried.

Perry felt like a fool. "It was a deer," he said. His eye

was tearing from the branch. He mopped at it angrily. "I'm sorry. I thought it was something."

"That's all right," Clay said. "It's better to make sure. You did the right thing."

"A deer!" Tim said. "I wish we'd had a gun. I'd go after him."

Perry said nothing, but when he remembered the proud, antlered head and the big liquid eyes, he was glad they had no gun.

They went back to the camp site and the rest of the night passed uneventfully, though in the morning when Tim went to the river to get the fish, they were gone.

chapter 22

"AN ANIMAL PROBABLY GOT THEM," TIM SAID.

"Or something," Perry said solemnly.

"Well, anyway," Clay said, "they're gone, and that means no breakfast."

"I could fish for some more," Tim said.

"We can't take the time. We'll get along all right until we break for camp. Let's get going."

The boys tried not to dwell on how hungry they were as they traveled on up the river, but toward noon they could think of little else.

"I guess we'd better try to find something to eat," Clay said. "We'll get weak. Tim, see if you can rassle up some fish."

But the fish were not biting. Tim patiently worked up and down the stream, concentrating on the rippled areas, but he had no luck. Perry found a blueberry patch and the boys ate hungrily, stripping the bushes, but berries were not enough to satisfy their hunger.

"We can't spend too much time here," Clay said. "I think we ought to go on. There may be better fishing farther on. Although fish alone aren't going to satisfy us very much."

Perry tried walking for a while until his ankle started paining, and then he had to get back on Chinook.

In the evening they camped near a sand bar that extended halfway across the river. The river was wider and deeper now, and Clay hoped that meant they were getting closer to the Spirit.

They were too tired and hungry to swim. Perry looked for greens, but he could find none he was sure of. Tim fished for a long time, but the best he could come up with was four small graylings. They cooked them and ate hungrily, feeling almost as hungry afterward. That night there was no singing around the campfire.

In the morning Tim went to untie the horses. He came back on the run. "The big footprint is there again," he said.

Clay and Perry hurried back with him. There, near the stallion, was the same strange huge footprint they had seen back in the canyon. They stared at it in silence.

"Why always just one?" Tim said.

"What could possibly make a track like that?" Perry asked. "There's nothing in the natural world . . ." He stopped as Clay looked at him. "Well, there isn't," he finished.

Clay knelt beside the print and examined it closely. He looked at the ground all around it. "Look," he said finally, "there's a faint print here."

"Another big one?"

"No, a regular footprint. Smooth, like a moccasin maybe, or a sneaker worn smooth. Like the ones we saw before." He got up. "I'm going to find out what's going on around here." He set off through the woods, his head bent toward the ground.

Perry and Tim went back and sat down. They talked for a while about what it might be, but nothing that either of them could think of made any sense.

"I'm too hungry to think," Tim said. "I'm going fishing."

"Clay said there should always be two of us here to watch the horses," Perry said.

"I'll just fish right out here off the sand bar. There's got to be fish in there somewhere." Tim got his pole and hook and line, and dug around in the ground until he found some worms. "Wish me luck."

Perry sat watching Tim. He pulled in the belt on his jeans. He knew he had lost weight, but that was all right with him; he had been plumper than he wanted to be. He wondered if he looked as different as he felt. It seemed to him that he had aged a couple of years on this trip. He wondered if his mother and father would notice the difference.

He looked up as Tim shouted, showing off a good-sized trout. Well, it was a start. Perry stretched out, dozed a little, and then came awake with a start. There was a noise in the woods. Before he became too alarmed, he saw that it was Clay, running toward them and holding something up.

"Look!" Clay called. "I found it!" Tim came running up from the river with his one trout. And Clay came up carrying some branches. He put them on the ground. "There is your giant footprint." The branches made the shape of a big print. "See where they've been tied together?" He pointed out the places where the branches had been bound together with rawhide.

"Somebody made it!" Tim said.

Clay nodded. "And hid it away after he used it. I found it stashed in some rocks."

"But who?" Perry said. "And what for?"

"Maybe to scare us," Clay said. "But who I don't know."

"I'll be darned," Tim said. "A bunch of tied branches." He looked relieved.

"Who did it?" Perry said.

"Whoever it is, I'm going to find him," Clay said. "I'm sick of this."

"How?" Perry asked.

"I don't know. I'll think of some way. Tim, let's cook that fish and then we'd better start out."

Again the fish, split three ways, was only an appetizer. Still hungry, they untied the horses, mounted, and set out. They rode for several hours and then stopped to make camp.

As they tied the horses, Clay said he'd take the midnight watch. "That's probably when he'll come around, if he's going to come at all."

"How do you plan to catch him?" Perry asked.

"I'll hide. He'll think we've all gone to sleep."

"Hey," Tim said, "we could stuff your jacket so it will look like you sleeping alongside us."

"Good idea," Clay said. He left to scout for food, and Tim went back to his fishing.

Perry found a patch of nettles nearby and picked them, but Tim had no luck with the fish.

Then Clay came back with a woodchuck. "I don't suppose it will be too tasty," he said, "but it's better than nothing."

"Thoreau ate one at Walden Pond," Perry said.

"Who's he?" asked Tim.

"Oh, this guy in New England who camped out for a couple of years."

"I didn't know you could camp out in New England," Tim said. "That's dude country."

"Of course you can," Perry said. "Anyway, this was over a hundred years ago."

When Clay had cooked the woodchuck, they sat down to eat it. It was tough and stringy, but as Perry said, beggars couldn't be choosers.

"That New England fellow must have been hard up for grub," Tim said.

But at least they had eaten meat, and they felt better.

Although Clay hid in the trees and stayed on watch longer than usual, nothing happened that night, except that once he thought he heard a strange kind of music. He woke the other boys to listen. They decided it was the wind in the trees.

chapter 23

TIM GOT UP EARLY BEFORE THE OTHERS AND WENT FISH-
ing. By the time Clay and Perry were awake, he had a
fire going and was cooking four trout. The delicious
smell woke Perry and even before his eyes were open,
he called out, "Fish!"

They divided the fish three ways, with a piece for
Bushman, and ate hungrily. Clay hurried them because
the sun was coming up hot again and he wanted to make
as much time as possible before it got too uncomfortable.

The flies were out in force. They settled on the horses
in clumps, especially around their eyes, and the mosquitoes droned around the boys. Small scratches from the
branches that brushed against them drew drops of blood
on the boys' faces and arms.

"I've got an idea," Tim said. He took off his shirt and
soaked it in the river. Then he buttoned it on so it draped
over his head and face and down over his shoulders, its
damp folds billowing out around him. He looked like
some strange animal or giant insect. "It works," he said,
his voice muffled.

Clay and Perry tried the same thing. Perry soaked his

T-shirt, too. He had his blue sweater tied by the arms around his waist. The T-shirt felt cool and good on his back until it began to dry out again.

"If only a breeze would come up," Perry said. But no one heard him. The horses switched their tails furiously, and Chinook rubbed her neck against Cloud. Cloud tried to rub against Storm, turning back and tossing her head this way and that, but Storm shied and snorted, and Clay had a difficult moment getting him quieted down again. The heat was hard on all of them. The horses looked unkempt. Even Chinook's usually glossy black coat was dull and streaked with dust. Her mane was full of broken twigs and burrs.

Perry leaned forward, peering out from under his shirt, trying to get some of them out for her, but she tossed her head and whinnied. Bushman walked alongside the horses, his tongue lolling out and his pace slow and tired. Now and then he loped away to investigate some chattering squirrel, but after a few minutes he gave up even that much unnecessary activity, and plodded along with his head down.

When the sun was high in the sky, Clay called a halt. "We'd better quit for a few hours and travel this evening. It's just too darned hot."

The boys dismounted with relief. Each one took a horse and led him to the river. Perry waded in first with Chinook. Chinook plunged her neck and head gratefully into the cool water and drank in great noisy gulps, tossing a spray of water over Perry. After a few minutes of drinking, she peered around at him to see what he was doing. He was sitting in the stream, holding her rope in one hand and splashing himself all over, clothes and all, with the other. She bent down and pushed him hard with her muzzle. He fell over backward. He was a little frightened—he was not entirely used to horses even yet. But he heard Clay and Tim laugh, so he laughed, too. After all, the water felt wonderful on the back of his neck.

Clay led Storm into the river, out into the middle. The stallion lay down on his side and rolled. The unexpected move pulled Clay off his feet and he, too, plunged into the water up to his neck. But he regained his feet quickly, in time to keep the restless stallion from breaking loose.

Cloud drank quietly, like a lady, watching the antics of the other two horses with a look of detachment. Tim scooped up handfuls of water and splashed them over her brown back until the streaks of dust disappeared. Her skin rippled under the touch of the water.

After they had tied up the horses in a place where they could graze on peavine, the boys took off their wet clothes and spread them on trees to dry. Then they splashed around in the blissfully cool water for a half hour or so.

Once dried off, they put on their still damp clothes, and moved back from the river to a place where the insects were not so thick.

Perry looked at the other two. "It's a good thing our parents can't see us now," he said. Their hair was long and matted and their faces were scratched and bitten. The left side of Tim's face was swollen from mosquito bites. Their clothes were damp and dirty. "We look like something, all right," he said. He wished he could see himself. He probably would never look like this again.

They lay under the trees and talked for a while, enjoying the luxury of stretching out straight. Then hunger stirred them to action. Clay went off to look for meat, and Perry set out to look for greens. Tim stayed to watch the horses, but he took his fishing pole down to the river's edge.

Perry circled around, not wanting to go far from the camping spot for fear of getting lost. Nearby he came to a burned-out area. Black stumps of trees stood ugly and grotesque, like figures in a nightmare. The area that had burned clear was covered with a pretty purple flower.

"Fireweed!" exclaimed Perry. With renewed energy he went to work picking it. He took off his shirt and filled it with the most tender stalks. There was spearmint growing nearby, and the pungent smell filled the sunshiny air. He picked some of that, too. Maybe he could make mint tea, if he could find something to use for tea. He remembered about Oswego tea, but he couldn't find any Oswego. Maybe he could make spruce tea, or they could just chew on the spearmint leaves—they were delicious. He came back happily with the load of treasure.

Tim had no luck fishing, and the mosquitoes and midges had finally driven him back from the river to the relative safety of the trees. The boys gathered wood and then they sat down to wait for Clay.

He was gone such a long time that they began to worry. Tim wouldn't admit that he was worried, but Perry noticed that he looked up every few minutes and stared into the woods in the direction that Clay had taken.

"Maybe he's lost," Perry said.

"Clay is too smart to get lost," Tim said. "Only dudes get lost."

"Like me, you mean," Perry said.

"I didn't say that." Tim grinned at Perry. "Listen, after this trip you won't be a dude anymore."

"I won't?" Perry was pleasantly surprised.

"We're pioneers, that's what we are," Tim said. "Hey, let's start the fire and cook that stuff you've got there. I'm starved."

"Me, too, but Clay has the matches," Perry said. Clay kept close track of the last of the precious matches they had found at the abandoned cattle ranch.

"That's right." Tim lay back. "Call me when he gets back." He closed his eyes.

Perry wished Tim wouldn't go to sleep, but he didn't want to say so. He busied himself cutting the greens into small stalks and then going down to the river to wash them. He filled the pot that he would cook them in and sat down again to chew on a spearmint leaf and wait for Clay.

If anything happened to Clay, they would never get home—he was sure of that. He wrapped his arms around his knees, shivering a little in spite of the heat. The longer he waited, the more alarmed he became. Finally he could sit still no longer. He got up and started to walk with some vague idea of meeting Clay.

He realized after a few minutes that he had walked out of sight of the horses—and Tim was asleep. How stupid! He turned back, but after a minute he became confused. He was not sure he was retracing his steps. The trees all looked alike. He was lost! He leaned against a tree, feeling almost too weak to stand.

Then he made himself straighten up. He couldn't just stand there and go to pieces. There had to be a way back.

The thing to do was to find the river. It couldn't be far away. He would walk a certain distance in each direction until he found it. He picked what seemed to be the likeliest way and started bravely off. He walked for several minutes, and found no sign or sound of the river, so he turned around and went back. Then it occurred to him that he was not sure he was going back exactly the way he had come. The thing to do was to get out his knife. He had seen Clay blaze trees—he would do that. He walked slowly, nicking a tree every few feet. When he got back to the point where he thought he had started, he made double nicks in a birch tree.

He started in the opposite direction, marking his progress. There was still no river. So he made his way back to the birch. In spite of not finding the river he was rather pleased with his system, and it seemed to him that he must find the river soon. But when he walked in a third direction, he came upon some of his blaze marks, and he realized that he had made a half circle. Now he was frightened. The blaze system wasn't working as well as it ought to. He got back to the birch and tried again. He came upon no more blaze marks, but neither did he come to the river.

Not only was he lost, but he had abandoned the horses while Tim slept. They might all be gone when he got back. He broke into a cold sweat. This time, when he got to the blazed birch, he stopped. He must keep cool. He must think. What would Clay do? Then a possible solution struck him. He could not be very far away from the camp. He opened his mouth wide and yelled.

Almost at once there was an answering yell. It was Tim. Nearly in tears with relief, Perry hurried toward the sound. "Keep yelling," he shouted.

Tim yelled at short intervals until Perry limped into the area where the horses were. They were still there. He joined Tim and sank down on the ground. "I was lost!"

"What were you doing out there?" Tim asked.

"Looking for Clay. But I couldn't find my way back, and I was afraid somebody would steal the horses while you were asleep."

"I wasn't really asleep," Tim said. "I heard you go."

They sat huddled close together in silence, waiting for Clay. And then, when it seemed they could hardly bear the suspense any longer, they heard Clay's voice.

He and Bushman came into sight. He was smiling broadly, and he was carrying something. He held it up as he came closer. It was a partridge.

"Food!" Tim yelled.

"And I found the Spirit River," Clay said. "At least I'm pretty sure it is. It's a real big river, and it looks like the Spirit. I found some caves, too, but I didn't dare take the time to explore them." He fished out the matches and lit the fire the boys had prepared. "Tonight we eat. To-morrow we hit the trail for home."

chapter 24

THERE WAS A BREEZE THE NEXT MORNING, AND THE HEAT and the bugs were not so troublesome. The boys traveled enthusiastically, well-fed for a change and eager to get to the Spirit River.

Clay broke through the brush and emerged with a shout at the point where the stream they had been following merged with a larger river.

"It's got to be the Spirit," Clay said. "It's so big and it's in the right place, the way I figure it. It's just got to be. We're probably a little north of Gold Reef, though, so let's follow it a ways south just to be sure."

"Yea, Spirit!" Tim slid off his horse and knelt beside the broad, fast-moving river, tossing up handfuls of water over his head. "Hurray!"

Perry got on Chinook and rode her into the water to drink. He rested his hands on her slender neck as she leaned down and gulped the water. He ducked as she tossed a spray of water over his head. "This doggone horse has a weird sense of humor," he said, but he was smiling broadly. He felt as if they were almost home. No water had ever looked so good to him as the rushing green water of the Spirit River.

After a few minutes of rest, they began what they hoped would be the last lap of their journey. With new strength they moved faster than they had done at any time since the beginning of their trip.

In the late afternoon they came to a small beaver meadow that swept away from the river up to a line of small hills, thickly forested.

"Let's camp at the foot of those hills," Clay said, "inside the wooded area. Then tomorrow morning we can cross the river and see if we can find Gold Reef." He dismounted from Cloud and ran with Bushman beside him until he came to a place he liked. "How about here for a camp?" he called. It was a grassy spot just inside the tree line. It was cool and still. The boys dropped their gear and tied up the horses. In the near distance the river glinted in the afternoon sun.

Bushman flopped on the ground, panting, but in a few minutes he caught sight of a small hare hopping off toward the nearest hill and he loped off after it.

The boys made camp and rested. Later Tim caught some fish and they had supper.

"Where's Bushman?" Perry asked.

Clay whistled, but the dog did not appear. "He's probably chasing rabbits," he said. He stretched out comfortably. "It's good to know we're really on the way home."

"You're sure we are?" Perry asked.

"About as sure as I can be. The land on the other side of the river looks familiar."

They prepared for sleep early, though Bushman still had not returned and Clay was a little worried. He walked out a way, whistling and calling, but there was no response.

He decided to take the first watch so he would be awake when Bushman came back. Tim went to sleep promptly, but Perry was too excited. He went and sat beside Clay in the shadows of a willow tree, talking about the next day's journey. With any luck they might make it to town before the day was over. They wondered if Joe had men out looking for them. He probably did.

Eventually Perry was thirsty and he went back to the campfire to get a drink, but the water was gone. So he decided to walk down to the river. He went quickly across the meadow, scared a rabbit, and as he watched it leap away, thought of Bushman and wished he would get back. At the river he lay down on his stomach beside the water and drank deeply. It tasted good, cold and clear. Before he could get up, Clay joined him for a drink.

The two got up together and started back. They were almost at the horses when they saw Chinook plunge forward and start to run in the opposite direction. They couldn't believe their eyes. Clay had tied her himself. Then, as she cleared the trees, they saw that there was

someone on her back, someone bent low over her neck.
Clay broke into a wild run. He shouted to Tim as he
passed him.

Perry jerked the tie rope loose and vaulted onto
Cloud's back. She was faster than Chinook, but Chinook
had a big head start. He dug his heels into Cloud's sides.
"Go, girl!" he shouted at her. She leaped forward into a

gallop in pursuit of the fleeing figure.

Whoever was riding Chinook headed her out across the meadow toward the river. Perry followed. The sky had clouded over and a wind had come up. It was half dark and Cloud's mane streamed in the wind. Once she stumbled in a gopher hole and nearly threw Perry. He saw the ground come frighteningly close. For a minute

he was afraid she had gone lame, but then she regained her stride. In the back of his mind he heard coyotes barking somewhere in the hills behind him. He tried to see who was riding Chinook, but the horses were going too fast. The wind whipped at his face and tossed his hair into his eyes. The figure on Chinook was still bent low over her neck, and he could get no clear view.

At the river Chinook slowed down and plunged into the water. She had disappeared into the woods on the other side by the time Perry got to the river. He urged Cloud into the water and when they had crossed, he slowed long enough to pick up the trail. He had to slow down again in the woods to keep from losing the tracks, but he kept going as fast as he could. Cloud was sure-footed and steady now, never shying as she used to do. She responded instantly to Perry's lightest touch.

It was dark in the woods and branches slashed at his face. He was badly scratched in a few minutes, but he did not want to slow down any more. He was determined to catch the creature who had been plaguing them for so long. The wind lifted limbs of trees and sent them cracking to the ground as if a giant hand were breaking them off. Once he narrowly missed being hit by a large branch that went hurtling past him to the ground.

Small animals skittered out of the way of the running horse, and somewhere an owl hooted. Once Perry caught sight of yellow eyes peering at him from the high branches of a tree.

Suddenly Chinook's tracks veered around and headed back toward the river. Perry turned Cloud in that direction. At the river's edge the tracks stopped. Perry rode across and picked them up again on the other side. The meadow had ended and the river was wooded on both sides now, and hilly on the side he had just reached. The hoofprints led up into the foothills. Perry rode hard now, Cloud's hoofs ringing out on the rock of the hills. Several times she slipped on loose shale and nearly plunged to the ground, but Perry pulled up her head and averted disaster.

Then they were in a dry wash. It ran alongside the hills for as far as he could see. There were no prints to be found on its loose gravel, but there was no indication that Chinook had come out of the gully on either side. The wash was straight and he could let Cloud out. They pounded down the middle of the gully and Perry strained to catch some sight of Chinook. Once he thought he saw her, but a heap of dead branches and brush in the wash took his attention. By the time he had guided Cloud around it, Chinook was gone again.

Now the wash went up over a rise in the ground and then down again. As Perry came down on the other side, he pulled Cloud to a stop so suddenly that she reared. There was an eight-foot barricade of logs and dead branches across the gully. He turned Cloud's head sharply to climb the bank and go around the barrier, but in that instant, out of the corner of his eye, he saw a figure leap from the top of the barricade straight at him. He felt himself struck and thrown from Cloud's back. He felt the ground rise up to meet him, sharp rocks digging into him. His head hit something hard and he lost consciousness.

chapter 25

WHEN PERRY CAME TO, HE WAS LYING IN THE BOTTOM OF the wash and Cloud was gone. He sat up. His head throbbed, and he felt blood on his cheek. He put his hand up gingerly and touched his head. There was a long gash on his forehead and it was still bleeding. He was badly bruised from the fall. He tried to get up, but he was so dizzy that he had to sit down again.

There was nothing to do but to sit quietly, trying to keep his head from spinning. But after a while he realized he would have to walk back to camp. It would take the boys a long time to find him, and, anyway, there was no point in waiting for them. He got up carefully and stood swaying. He felt terrible. Not only was he hurt, but they had lost all the horses except Storm, and even Bushman was missing. And he was no closer to solving the mystery than ever. Whoever it was had just ambushed him from the pile of logs. Chinook must have been out of sight on the other side. He had ridden right into the trap.

He took a step forward and stopped. There, in the dirt and gravel at his feet, was a sign. It was the shape of a turtle, drawn in the dirt and outlined with stones. Perry shivered. What did it mean? Then he kicked at it in anger. He was not going to be frightened by a stupid collection of stones and a few lines drawn in the dirt with a stick. It was just some crazy kind of superstition, meant to frighten him. Well, he would not be frightened.

He walked slowly up the dry wash, keeping his eyes on a stump straight ahead of him to avoid dizziness. His head pounded painfully. He wondered if he had a concussion and what you were supposed to do about it.

After what seemed a very long time, he came to the place where they had entered the wash. Laboriously he climbed up a short slope onto the grassy bank. Then, in a moment, he was in the woods. He stopped often to lean against a tree and wait for his head to clear. He longed to lie down, but he knew he must get back to camp.

In time he came to the river. There was no need to follow the tracks now. He stayed on the side of the stream where he was and made his way along it. Just then he heard a shout and a great splashing. He jerked his head up and felt the blinding pain that came with the sudden movement.

It was Clay and Tim running to meet him. They had been following the tracks on the other side of the river. They ran heedlessly through the water, Tim almost falling on the wet stones.

"Boy! we thought you'd gone clear to China!" Tim

said. "Where have you been? What happened to your head?"

"Where's Cloud?" Clay asked.

Perry sat down, leaned against a tree, and closed his eyes. Briefly he told them what had happened. They were silent for a moment. Then Tim said, "We got to get you back to camp, Perry, so you can be taken care of. You look terrible. Clay, you prop him up one side, and I'll take the other."

The two boys looped Perry's arms over their shoulders and hoisted him to his feet. Half carrying him they finally got him back to camp.

They laid him gently on the ground, and Clay put his sweater over him. He got some water and carefully washed the gash in his head.

"There's some gauze pads and adhesive in my knapsack," Clay said. Tim got them and made a patch for the cut.

"That's a real bad cut," Tim said. "I wouldn't be surprised if you had a concussion. You better just take it easy for a while."

Perry asked the question that had been on his mind. "Did Bushman come back?"

"No," Tim said. "I thought I heard him barking once, but when I went to look for him, I couldn't find a trace."

Perry closed his eyes. Things had turned out badly all around. He wished he could sleep.

"What do you think it was that got you?" Tim looked fearful.

"I don't know. I kept catching glimpses of Chinook streaking across the meadow. The thing on his back looked like . . . like . . ." Perry paused and shuddered. ". . . like the headless horseman."

Tim's eyes widened. "What's that?"

Perry closed his eyes. "Just something in fiction. Not real. I don't know what it was, Tim."

"I wonder if it'll come back for Storm?"

"It doesn't matter too much, I guess. One horse isn't much to show for all our trouble. Joe will be awfully disappointed."

"Well, we tried," Tim said.

The boys sat in silence for a long time. Tim got up and replenished the fire. "Why don't you get some sleep, Perry? I'll stand watch."

"All right," Perry said. But he couldn't sleep. There were too many things to think about, and his head ached too much.

Nothing unusual occurred that night.

Next morning Perry slept, waking now and then to ask for a drink of water. Each time he waked, he asked if Bushman was back. They had to tell him no. Perry felt terrible about Chinook, too. He had spent so much time on the mare's back that he had come to feel very close to her. He missed her funny little tricks and the way she had of rubbing her upper lip against his hand.

Later in the day Perry got up. He felt like moving around. His head was better. It was early evening, and still light, so he took the hatchet and set out to see if he could find some greens. He stayed within sight and sound of the river so he wouldn't get lost, prowling mostly along the edge of the woods within hailing distance of the camp. Tim and Clay were in camp watching Storm.

Suddenly he heard a rustling in the brush. At once it came to his mind that it might be the enemy, and he froze. But in a moment a small porcupine waddled into sight. Perry was relieved and excited. Here was something he could kill with the hatchet. He hit the porcupine with the blunt edge though he hated to do it; it didn't seem right to kill things. But they had to eat. He hit it again to make sure he had killed it, and the porcupine lay still. Perry turned it over with his foot while he got out his knife. He would have to skin it to carry it back. He had seen Clay skin the one that Bushman brought home and following that pattern he made a careful slit down the middle of the belly and folded the skin back. It made him feel queasy, but he did it. Carefully he removed the hide, surprised to find that it was so easy to do.

Triumphant now and already forgetting how bad he felt, he picked up the body of the animal and ran back to camp. It was the first time he had tried running since he hurt his ankle. It hurt some, but not enough to stop him. "Look!" he cried. "Porcupine!"

Clay was sitting by the fire, talking to Tim, when Perry brought the porcupine. Both boys shouted with glee, and Clay showed Perry how to cook the meat.

There was not as much of it as they could have eaten, but it helped to ward off hunger. It tasted even better and more tender than the bigger one that Bushman had caught.

"In the morning," Clay said, "I'm going to hunt for Bushman and Chinook."

"What if we get lost again?" Perry said. "We're so close to home."

"I won't get lost," Clay said. "But I've got to find them, especially Bushman." He lowered his head to hide the emotion he felt about his dog.

"We ought to be able to track Chinook," Tim said.

Clay nodded. "Only if he's been ridden clear away, they've got such a big start we might never catch up."

"Well, we'll give it a try," Tim said. He went down to the river to wash the cooking dishes.

Later that night, when the half-dark had closed in, and Tim was on watch, Clay woke up. After a while he sat up and said to Perry, "I'm going for a little walk."

"I'll go with you," Perry said.

"I keep thinking I hear a dog barking. It's probably just a coyote, but I want to check it out."

"Tell Tim. We won't go far. I'm too jittery to sleep."

"Take the hatchet," Perry said.

They walked back along the river, keeping close to the woods. Every few minutes they stopped and listened. There were many night sounds. They heard a wolf howl, and Clay wondered if that was what he had heard instead of Bushman. But he was sure it was not.

They came up to the highest of the hills that bordered the area and stopped again to listen. There the birds were already starting their morning racket. By this time Perry's head was aching badly and he decided if they didn't hear anything, he would go back and wait till morning.

Then they did hear something, but it wasn't barking.

It was the strange, eerie music they had heard once before, like the thin, lonely music of a flute, only it was unlike any real music they had ever heard. They had thought before that it was the wind in the trees, but now there was no wind.

They listened with all their attention. It was in a minor key and it seemed to drift like smoke over the tops of the trees and hills. It was impossible to tell what direction it came from. They stood still for a long time, listening. It made Perry feel lonely and afraid.

Then, unmistakably, they heard a dog barking. Clay was sure it was Bushman. But the bark sounded hollow and faraway. They could not place its direction. Clay called and whistled and after he did, both the barking and the music stopped. With that Clay climbed the hill and went down the other side and around the base back to where he had started. He found nothing.

Then Perry's head began to hurt so badly that he had to sit down and lean his forehead on his arms. He was very dizzy, and the world kept spinning and turning black.

"Are you all right?" asked Clay.

"I'll be all right in a minute," Perry said. "We've got to find Bush." He tried to get up, but he staggered and Clay caught him.

"Perry, you've got to go back and rest," Clay said. "I've taken you too far. You look terrible. Tim and I will look for Bushman in the morning. If he's barking he must be somewhere close."

"He must be trapped," Perry said, "or he'd come."

"We'll find him. Don't worry." Clay took a firm grip on Perry's elbow. "Come on back now."

Reluctantly Perry let Clay help him back to the camp site. They came out of the woods and crossed a strip of meadow and approached camp. Clay called to Tim, but there was no answer. They could see Storm grazing quietly.

"Tim shouldn't have gone off and left Storm," Clay said.

"Maybe he fell asleep," Perry said.

They brushed past the trees into the little clearing and stopped short. Tim was gone. The fire was flaming high, throwing shadows over the clearing, and everything that belonged to them had been piled on the fire. Knapsack, cooking utensils. Clay's jacket, everything was in flames. There were hoofprints all around the clearing. The two boys stood staring in disbelief as the fire lit up their faces.

chapter 26

"TIM'S GONE!" PERRY CRIED OUT.

Clay looked around quickly. "Let's go," he said. "We've got to find him."

"How?"

"Follow the horse's tracks." Clay kicked at the fire and knocked his flaming knapsack out. It was charred and blackened. "Nothing left," he said. "Not a thing." He started running in the path of the horse's hoofs, but turned back to say, "You'd better stay here. Take it easy."

"I'm coming, too," Perry said, his head forgotten.

The trail was clear enough. It led back toward the hills. As they went into the woods, the prints were fainter, but they were still there in the trodden pine needles. Branches were freshly broken.

Soon they came into another clearing. "Look," Perry said. He pointed in the opposite direction. There was a plume of smoke rising lazily into the air.

Clay studied it for a moment. "It can't be whoever it is we're following," he said. "It's in the wrong direction. It must be trappers or somebody."

"We could get them to help us," Perry said.

"It's too far away. There isn't time." Clay started off again. Perry had to run hard to keep up with him. He was panting, and once he had to call to Clay to wait for him.

Then, so abruptly that Perry almost bumped into him, Clay stopped.

"What is it?" Perry said.

Clay pointed to the hoofprints. They stopped short at the sheer face of a hill that ran almost straight up and down. The boys looked up. It was impossible for even a rabbit to climb that cliff.

"Listen!" Perry said.

"What?"

They stood still a moment. Then, echoing hollowly, came Bushman's bark.

"Bushman!" Clay shouted. He whistled. "Bush!"

The barking began again. It seemed both near and faraway.

Clay began poking frantically at the face of the hill.

"What are you doing?" Perry asked.

"It must be a cave," Clay said. "Help me find it."

Perry prodded the hillside with his hands, but he was worried. "It may not be Bushman at all; it may be a trap."

"I'd know Bushman's bark anywhere," Clay said. Then he shouted, "I found it!" He pulled aside some brush that had been carefully placed over the mouth of the cave.

"My gosh!" Perry said, "It's big."

The opening was about six feet high and three feet across. Clay stepped toward it and disappeared from sight.

"Clay!" Anxiously Perry stuck his head in. Clay was standing just inside. It was so dark that Perry could hardly see him. "Are you going in there?"

"I've got to go after Bushman," Clay said. "And Tim must be in here, too."

"It's a trap," Perry said.

"Maybe. But we can't just do nothing." He unbuckled the small flashlight that hung from his belt. "This isn't much good, but it's better than nothing. Stay right behind me and be careful where you step."

The first faint beam of the flashlight picked out a small circle of light on the floor of the cave. It was covered with dead vegetation and broken twigs. Clay stepped forward carefully. "Hold on to my belt," he said. "Be careful of loose rocks." His voice sounded flat.

Perry clung to Clay's belt. He couldn't see the circle that the flashlight lit up. The sides of the cave's entrance pressed close to him and he felt as if there was no air. He had the frightening sensation of not being able to breathe. The atmosphere was deathly cold and dank.

They moved forward very slowly. Several times Clay slipped on loose rock and nearly fell. The sides of the cave narrowed and then widened. Everything seemed wet and the boys could hear the slow drip of water somewhere. Perry felt something move under his foot and he realized with horror that it was a snake. He stepped forward so quickly that he bumped into Clay.

"It was a snake," he said.

"No poisonous snakes up here," Clay said. "Watch your head."

Perry ducked just in time to miss a sharp shelf of rock. He tried to concentrate on what was at hand and not to think about what lay in store for them. He dared not think about poor Tim, or about his own aching head.

Clay stopped. "There's a place here we've got to navigate very carefully," he said. He felt along the rock wall with his hand, and played the light over the surface. "Look here." He flattened back against the rock so Perry could see. There was a narrow shelf of rock about a foot wide, with a drop on the far side of it that went down into a seven-foot-deep cavern.

Perry gasped. "We can't get by that."

"Yes, we can," Clay said firmly. "Just hold onto me now." He held out his free hand and grabbed Perry by the wrist. "Don't look down." He angled the light back so Perry could see the ledge. "Get your feet up against the wall and keep them pressed against it all the way."

Perry closed his eyes for a moment. "All right," he said faintly.

"We'll take it slow," Clay said. He took a step forward.

Perry shuffled his feet forward, keeping them so hard against the rocks that the pressure hurt his bones. Moving very slowly and holding tight to Clay's hand, he inched forward. After what seemed like years, he heard Clay say, "We made it." Perry leaned against the wall, weak with relief.

They were in a big chamber now and their footsteps echoed hollowly. They picked their way carefully through the loose rock. "Watch it," Clay said suddenly. "There's a stalactite." He veered sharply to one side. Perry put out his hand and touched the hard, damp stalactite. "My goodness," he said. He had been in some caves once in Bermuda with his parents, and he had seen stalactites and stalagmites, but this seemed more real somehow.

He cried out in alarm as something whooshed past his face. "What was it?"

"Just a bat," Clay said.

"*Just* a bat!" Perry shuddered. Then he found that he had started shivering and couldn't stop. It was terribly cold.

Clay stopped again. "There are two different ways we can go ahead," he said. "We would get lost in here and never get out!"

"Maybe we should go back," Perry said.

"And leave Tim?"

"No. Of course not. We can't do that."

Clay stood still for a moment, playing the light over

the walls. They were black and slimy. "We need to leave some kind of trail so we can find our way back."

"How? You can't blaze a trail on rock."

"You're the great reader. Remember the story of the minotaur?"

"A thread!" Perry said. "But we don't have any thread."

"We can use your sweater."

"My mother will kill me," Perry groaned.

"Better than dying in a cave." Clay held out his hand. Perry took off the sweater and gave it to him. He shivered more violently than ever. But Clay was in his shirtsleeves, too. His jacket was ashes, back in the fire. Clay got out his knife and cut a thread in the sweater and began to unravel it. When he had a ball of loose yarn in his hand, he tied one end to a stalactite and said, "Here we go." Perry took hold of Clay's belt again and they went on.

"I'm just picking this way by chance," Clay said. "We may come up against a blank wall."

They moved along in silence for a while. The passageway narrowed again and at one point they had to squeeze their way through. Perry again felt he could not possibly breathe. A jagged rock tore his T-shirt and scratched him.

When they came into a wider place, Clay stopped again. "I wish Bushman would bark," he said. And just as he said it, Bushman's bark echoed through the cave.

It seemed to be close by, and it sounded eerie.

"Come on," Clay said. He pushed forward eagerly.

In a few minutes they squeezed their way into a small chamber, and there was Bushman jumping all over them and giving little yips of joy. Over their heads they could see a spot of daylight through the hole he had made when he fell in.

"He must have chased a rabbit and fallen through," Clay said. "Watch it, Bush, don't break our thread." One sleeve of Perry's sweater was gone.

There was another very narrow place on the far side of the chamber. The boys squeezed through it and Clay boosted Bushman through. Bushman had to lie down and inch his way forward. Finally they were clear of that passageway and into a wider place. They went on slowly.

It was bitter cold and Perry's teeth chattered. He put his hand into Bushman's shaggy coat and felt the dog's warmth. It was comforting.

They had to kneel and crawl through a small hole in the rocks. It was difficult to get Bushman through, but Clay pulled and Perry pushed. Then the three of them stood upright in the biggest chamber they had yet come to. Clay's flashlight was getting fainter, but he flashed it slowly around the chamber. There were rock ledges above their heads.

Clay played the light past a corner of the room and then brought it back again. "Tim!"

Perry strained his eyes to see. It was Tim, all right. He was lying on the floor, bound and gagged. Clay started toward him.

"Stop!" It was a deep voice above their heads, and it echoed through the cavern like a peal of thunder. The boys froze. They strained their eyes and Clay played his light over the ledges, but they saw nothing.

"Drop your flashlight!" The voice seemed to come from directly over them, but that was impossible.

"Who are you?" Clay's voice was strained.

There was a swoop of light and there, on a ledge above and in front of them, stood a weird figure. He was holding a flaming torch above his head and in his other hand he held a gun. The face of the creature was blackened and the bones were outlined in white paint. It was a fantastic face.

"I am Falling Star," said the echoing voice, "son of a chief."

"Falling Star, son of a chief," Clay said, making his voice deep and loud, "what do you want with us?"

"You have taken my trapping grounds. These have been my trapping grounds and my fathers' for many generations of our tribe. The white man has stolen them."

"We are not trappers," Clay said. Under the cover of the darkness he handed the unravelled sweater to Perry. Bushman kept growling deep in his throat, but Clay kept his hand on his collar.

"The white man has taken my hunting ground. I warned white man in village before. Still white man comes back. He must pay for it." The Indian brandished the torch and the sparks flew up around his head. "Put down your light."

Clay dropped the flashlight onto the floor. It made a hollow clatter.

"Now turn around."

The boys turned slowly.

"Keep turning. Faster! Faster!" There was a loud report and a bullet ricocheted off the floor close to Clay's feet. The boys revolved faster. Perry felt dizzy. He put out a hand to steady himself. If he had not had the sight of the Indian to orient himself, he would not have known which end of the cavern they had entered.

"Faster!" cried the voice. Suddenly the torch went out and they were plunged into darkness and silence.

They stopped whirling. Perry had to lean over and put his hands on the floor to steady himself. Clay bumped into him.

"I'm looking for Tim," Clay murmured.

There was a snuffling sound as Bushman sought out Tim.

"He's here," Clay said in a low voice.

Perry couldn't see him in the almost total blackness, but he put out his hand and felt Clay's arm as Clay snapped open his knife and cut Tim's bonds.

"Thanks." Tim's voice sounded muffled.

"Grab Perry's belt and keep quiet," Clay said. He guided Perry's hand to his own belt. "Give me the yarn," he said softly. Perry gave it to him, and they began to move, walking softly.

So it was an Indian, Perry thought. He felt the tug of Tim's fingers on his belt as they moved slowly back along the path they had come. He had no doubt that the Indian was watching them in the darkness. He wouldn't know about the yarn and would expect them to get lost. If Clay hadn't been so smart, they would have gotten lost. This place was a real labyrinth. The question now was what the Indian would do when he discovered they had found their way out. They were three, plus Bushman, to one, but the Indian had a gun.

They moved slowly, in total darkness most of the way, guided by the thread and by what they remembered. It seemed ages before they came to the place where the thread was tied, and then they had to grope their way to the narrow ledge. Perry shivered with fear and cold. He hated having to walk that thing again, even if the cavern below them was only seven feet deep.

He felt Clay flatten against the rock wall and move cautiously out onto the ledge. He took a deep breath and followed, signaling to Tim to be careful. He heard a rock clink against another behind them. It was not Tim's feet that had dislodged the rock! The sound came from too far behind them. It had to be the Indian, right on their trail. Why had they thought he would ever let them out of there alive?

Perry felt Tim's fingers disengage themselves from his belt. What was he up to? Perry moved his hand back to where Tim ought to be, but there was only space, and nothing for Perry to do but to follow Clay across the ledge. Perry was worried. He didn't know whether to risk speaking to Clay or not. The Indian knew where they were anyway . . .

There was a scream and a crash.

"Tim!" Clay's voice sounded flat in the cave. He and Perry had reached the far side of the ledge.

"I'm O.K.," Tim's voice said. "Grab my feet, Perry. I'm right below you. I got to get that gun."

Perry wanted to ask questions, but he seized Tim's feet and held on. In a moment Tim handed up the gun to Clay. Then he scrambled up himself. There was a sound of moaning below them.

"Is the Indian down there?" Perry asked.

"Yes. I shoved him off the ledge. I don't think he's hurt bad. It's not much of a drop." He raised his voice. "Falling Star, come up out of there."

There was a louder groan.

"Are you hurt?" Clay asked. They were close enough to the entrance that there was a little light now. Clay leaned over the edge trying to see, and so did Perry. Dimly he could make out a figure huddled in the bottom of the cavern. Bushman whined and pawed the floor. Clay handed the gun to Tim and reached down. "Grab my hand, Falling Star. And don't try any tricks. We've got the gun."

With many groans and outcries, the Indian let Clay pull him up to the floor of the cave.

"I've got him," Clay said. He took the gun from Tim and prodded the Indian. "Out."

Bushman growled continuously in his throat, but Clay said, "It's all right, boy. We've got him."

In a few minutes they were through the mouth of the cave. The sunlight seemed almost unbearably bright and wonderfully warm, but even so, Perry could not stop shivering.

In the daylight, without his torch and his high ledge, the Indian looked small and scrawny. His painted face was grotesque, but no longer frightening. He seemed afraid of them. Perry felt almost sorry for him.

"What you do with Falling Star?" the Indian asked in a faint voice.

"We'll see," Clay said.

Tim was rubbing his arms and legs to get back the circulation where he had been tied up. "Clay, he's got five of our horses. Unless he's lying, he says he has them in a corral up in back of this hill."

"Let's go and see," Clay said. He poked the Indian with the barrel of the gun. "Lead the way."

"What about Storm?" Perry asked.

"We'll get him on the way back."

Meekly the Indian walked on ahead of them, around

the curve of the hill.

"Look," Clay said, pointing to something that hung from the Indian's belt. "He's got my compass."

"He's got a flute," Tim said. "That was the sound we heard once, remember? And he told me he made the landslide."

As they came into open land, the Indian pointed. In the distance was a crude corral and there were the horses. Clay gave a shout of joy.

The boys hurried toward them. "There's plenty of rope," Clay said. "We can get them into town all right."

"What you do with Falling Star?" the Indian asked again.

"First you can help us get into town. You know the way. And no funny business," Clay said sternly. "Then we'll see."

They got the horses out of the corral and set off for town, Clay and Falling Star leading the way, Perry and Tim bringing up the rear.

chapter 27

Joe sat with his leg propped up on a chair. It was in a full-length cast. The boys sat on the floor around him.

"I sure was worried about you fellers," he said. "I came back up here to look for you and you hadn't showed up. I had John Blake out scouring the countryside. But all he found was four horses."

"We saw his smoke once," Clay said, "but we didn't have time right then to follow it."

"Well, you'll have something to tell your folks." Joe smiled down at them. "And you can tell them pretty soon now. The truck is fixed, and Pete Blake has offered to drive us down, just for the ride. We're in luck." They were sitting in the living room of Hi Fuller's house in Gold Reef. Outside in Hi's corral were the ten horses. Joe reached down and rubbed Bushman's ear. "It may be a mite crowded, but after all you been through, it's going to seem like heaven."

"I wonder what Falling Star is doing now," Perry said. "He must be kind of lonesome without us."

"Around here we call him Indian Tom," Hi Fuller

said. "The Mountie read him the riot act. He should mind his manners for a while. He could have been locked up for all he did to you. We've had trouble with him before. That land you were on used to belong to his tribe. He figures it still does."

"They say he's not quite right in the head," Joe said, "but he wouldn't have harmed you."

Clay shook his head. "I'm not so sure of that."

"Anyway, you're safe," Joe said. "And you proved to one Indian that a man who keeps his wits about him wins out."

"Wits," Perry said. "Clay kept his wits all right, but me, I panicked every hour on the hour."

"Listen," Tim said, "you were kind of nervous at first, but you were doing real good there at the end."

Perry flushed with pleasure. He pulled a pile of blue yarn from his pants pocket. "Wait till my mother sees my sweater."

"Wait till you tell her about the Indian," Tim said, "a real, live hostile Indian."

"Wait till she hears how he painted his face," Perry said.

"And how he stood up there with his old torch, like the Statue of Liberty," Tim said, "and bellowed 'My name is . . .'"

"The Spirit of Christmas Past," Perry said. Both boys doubled over with laughter.

Clay grinned at Joe. "It wasn't so much the Indian,"

he said, "or the dangers of the forest as it was these madmen I had to travel with."

Perry laughed. He got up and went out on the porch. Tim and Clay followed him. The moon was just coming up over the wooded mountains, and there was a bright, broad path of moonlight on the river.

"You know," Clay said, "I'm going to miss this country."

The boys looked at each other and nodded. This, they knew, was an adventure they would never forget.